DEATH OVER MONTREAL

Geoffrey Bilson

the **Kids Canada** series

Goodbye Sarah
by Geoffrey Bilson

A Proper Acadian
by Mary Alice Downie and George Rawlyk

The Tin-Lined Trunk
by Mary Hamilton

The King's Loon
by Mary Alice Downie

Death Over Montreal

by Geoffrey Bilson

Kids Can Press • Toronto

This publication was produced with the generous assistance of The Canada Council and The Ontario Arts Council.

Canadian Cataloguing in Publication Data

Bilson, Geoffrey, 1938-
Death over Montreal

(Kids Canada series, ISSN 0227-3144)
ISBN 0-919964-45-1

I. Title. II. Series.

PS8553.I47D42 jC813'.54 C82-094849-7
PZ7.B44De

Cover illustration by M. Cserepy and W. Taylor.

Printed in Canada by
The Alger Press Limited

Kids Can Press, Toronto

For my son Max and our old friend Hound.

Chapter One

THE roar of the anchor cable woke Jamie Douglas. "We've arrived at last," he thought. "Six weeks from Glasgow to Canada." He propped himself on his elbow and looked around the ship's hold. In the faint light he could see the rows of berths stacked one above the other. Each berth held a family and Jamie had grown used to the noise of crying babies and the stench of people living so close together.

For days they had lived with the ports closed and the hatches down as the ship rolled and tossed its way through Atlantic storms. Two babies had died and the only thing that had kept Jamie's spirits high was his father's tales of the new life they would make in Canada.

Now they had arrived and were lying at anchor. Jamie was eager to see the harbour. He groped in the straw for his boots and slipping between the boxes and bundles he climbed up to the deck.

The dawn air felt fresh and crisp. Jamie stepped quickly to the rail and peered through the fog toward the shore. In the distance he could see a hilly island with a cluster of sheds around a flag pole. There were crowds of people milling around the buildings and here and there the scarlet coat of a soldier, but nothing appeared to be happening. The settlement was small and as grey as the morning; not at all the way Mr. Douglas had described.

"Is that Quebec?" Jamie asked the ship's mate, who was standing near him.

"Och no lad," said the mate, roaring with laughter, "you've no cause to sound so downhearted. It's just Grosse Isle. We're here under orders. It seems the damned cholera's got here ahead of us. We canna' go to Quebec before stopping here for the quarantine."

Cholera! Jamie felt a shiver run through his body. He knew the only reason his mother had agreed to leave Scotland was to escape the disease. It was new and terrible and by 1830 had spread from India, across Europe to Great Britain, killing thousands of people as it passed. No one could stop it. No one could cure it.

"Now lad," said the mate, "with God's help, you've come through some mighty storms to get here. You should leave yourself in His hands now that you're here. There's always more that live than die in these affairs."

Jamie could think only of his mother. Her hopes would be dashed. He couldn't be the one to tell her.

He turned away and looked over the water. Small boats, weighted down with passengers, were moving toward the shore. The boats bobbed in the heavy swell at the water's edge and people were tossed in every direction.

"That'll be the doctor," the mate said, nudging Jamie and pointing to a boat that was pulling up alongside the *Jane*. "Best be getting everyone up to meet him."

Slowly, people began to emerge from the hold. Jamie watched for his parents. When they appeared, he joined them by the main mast.

The doctor, hampered by his heavy cloak, made a clumsy business of climbing the rope ladder. He had a short conversation with the ship's master as the last immigrants struggled up from the hold.

"Very well now," the doctor called, "Captain MacAlister tells me there's been no sickness on board. That's good, but I'll have to take a look at all of you before you are allowed any further."

"What's it all about?" shouted someone in the crowd.

"Regulations! All passengers, baggage, and vessels must be cleaned before going up river. You'll be quarantined on Grosse Isle."

"But we're all healthy. Why do we have to waste our time?"

"The Board of Health requires it since the cholera..." The doctor's words were lost in a rush of voices. Jamie could feel panic sweep through the group. He turned to his mother. Her face was white. The mate might tell him to trust in God, but a lot of people who had done so were dead.

The doctor was shouting to be heard. "No, no. I've no time to waste here. Just line up so that I can look at you all."

The sailors began to push people into line and the doctor walked along looking at tongues and stopping occasionally to ask questions or to examine someone more closely.

"Very well," he said at last, "everything seems to be in order. Gather your belongings and make your way to the Island. Expect to spend at least one night there."

There was little time to brood as they prepared for the short trip. The ship's deck was teaming with families struggling to stay together with their possessions. The Douglases all managed to get into one boat, along with their few bags.

When they arrived on shore, a soldier directed them up a worn path that led from the beach. A man in a Sergeant's uniform was standing at the top of the hill giving orders.

"This way," he shouted. People struggled with their boxes and bags and stumbled up the hill toward the Sergeant.

"Come along now, come along. Hurry ... hurry ... pick up your feet, step lively. There's hundreds more to come, no time to waste. Clothing's to be washed over there and dried before repacking. You may shelter in the sheds there behind me ... but no fighting, cursing, or undue noise. Take my word and keep an eye on your things. There's thieves among you. Now, carry on."

Mr. Douglas led them to the top of the hill. From there they could see a small bay where, all along the shore, women were washing clothes. In some places they were shoulder to shoulder, and the water at their feet was thick and scummy.

"Do you see a place, Mary?" Mr. Douglas asked.

"I'll make one, don't you worry. Now, bring the baggage."

Jamie and his father followed Mrs. Douglas into the cove. She pushed her way towards the water.

"Stay here and help your mother, Jamie. I'm away to look things over." Mr. Douglas strode off briskly.

Jamie watched him go. "It's always the same with him," he thought, "he's away from the hard work."

In his twelve years, Jamie could not remember a time when his father was not on the move. Each new job was to be the one that would change everything. But for Jamie the change meant a new house, new friends and a new school. For the last three years they had lived in Glasgow and kept a shop. Mrs. Douglas did the work while Mr. Douglas chatted amiably with the customers. Then one day he had decided to emigrate.

"One last move, Mary," Mr. Douglas had promised, "a big one, a fresh start where I can make a go of things. And Jamie — why he can do anything, the prospects are so great."

So these were the great prospects! Jamie and his mother doing the work, while Mr. Douglas was looking for opportunity.

Chapter Two

JAMIE sat in the hot afternoon sun, half-sleeping and half-watching the drying laundry. He wasn't aware of the young red-haired boy who was working his way along the shore. The boy came up behind Jamie, and after quickly looking around, snatched one of Mr. Douglas's shirts. The shirt was a fine linen one with lace at the collar and cuffs, and Mr. Douglas had refused to sell it before they left Scotland.

Jamie was puzzled for a moment until he realized that the boy thought he was asleep and was stealing the shirt.

Jamie scrambled to his feet. "Hey, what are you doing?" he shouted, expecting the boy would drop the shirt. But the boy just turned, looked at him defiantly, and then raced off. Jamie took off after him.

People watched the two boys but no one tried to stop the thief as he ran up the hill. Jamie ran as fast as he could but his lungs burned and he felt his legs growing heavy. He would never have caught the thief had the boy not tripped over a rock. Jamie was beside him before he could scramble to his feet again.

"That's my shirt, give it to me," Jamie declared.

The boy stood up and spat. "'Tis not your shirt, 'tis me father's own shirt. Me mother sent it to him from the washing grounds. She said he's to look fine and grand."

Jamie looked around for someone to help. "That's a lie and you know it."

"What's the trouble, boys?" asked a man who had stepped out from the small crowd that was gathering around.

"He stole my father's shirt, sir," said Jamie angrily.

"I did not. 'Tis me father's shirt," the boy yelled back.

"Only one way to settle this. You'll fight; the winner takes the shirt."

"But it's my shirt and he stole it." Jamie couldn't believe what was happening.

"I'll fight for it," the boy said eagerly.

The boys were quickly surrounded by a circle of spectators. Someone helped Jamie take off his coat and shirt. All around, Jamie could hear men betting on the fight. As the red-haired boy stripped, Jamie saw that he was small but well muscled. Jamie was suddenly self-conscious of his own scrawny chest and spindly legs and arms.

"A shilling on the red-head, what odds on the tall one?" came a call.

Jamie felt worse when he heard the gamblers betting on his opponent. He tensed as he watched the other boy balancing on his toes and swinging his arms to loosen the muscles.

"I'd rather be anywhere else on earth," he thought, looking at the ring of eager faces that surrounded him.

The referee called the boys to the centre of the circle. "Fair fight boys, no kneeing, biting, or scratching. Round ends when one of you falls. There's a minute to come up." With his boot heel, he made a line between them and stepped back.

The two boys circled each other, the red-haired boy grinning confidently. Jamie's only chance would be to try to surprise him. He would go in fast and catch him off guard.

Jamie rushed ahead, forcing himself to keep his eyes open. He caught the other boy full in the stomach, and followed with a series of blows. He stepped back to catch his breath, but when he looked up the boy was grinning the same confident, mocking grin.

"Now, is that all a big boy like you can do? Why don't you hit me here, right on me chin," and he pushed his chin out.

The crowd laughed and Jamie grew angry. He rushed forward again, determined to punch the boy on the chin, but the red-head stepped forward and struck Jamie in the stomach. Jamie doubled up and then sprawled on the ground, winded and sick.

"End of the round," called the referee.

Jamie was able to come to the line for the next round, though there seemed to be little point to it. The round lasted only as long as his opponent wanted it to. Jamie hoped to hold the boy back by using his longer reach, but a quick step brought the boy inside Jamie's guard where the red-head hit him at will before sending him sprawling again. Jamie lay still for a moment, then rolled over and came up onto his knees.

The third round went no better than the others. Most of the crowd had drifted away, bored by the unequal match. Only the bettors stayed for the finish. Jamie hoped that the referee would call a halt so he could at least feel that he had come out for every round. The man showed no sign that he would and now, even the red-head himself seemed to grow bored with the fight. His mood changed and the mocking look disappeared from his face. He came straight at Jamie and kicked him in the stomach, then butted him with his head. The crowd and the trees spun and faded into blackness. Jamie went down.

When Jamie came to, he was flat on his back, aching and barely able to breath through his bloodied nose. He rolled his head to one side. The crowd had gone, except for a tall man who was taking money from one of the bettors. The man turned and looked coldly at Jamie before walking off. Jamie tried to sit up, but his head throbbed. He lay down again, closing his eyes tightly, afraid that he might start to cry.

"Just lie there awhile, I've brought you some water." Someone was wiping his face and chest with a cool, wet cloth, using it gently around the cuts and bruises.

Jamie opened his eyes, and turned his head to look at his helper. A girl, a few years older than he, was kneeling beside him.

She pressed the cloth to the bruise on his head. "How do you feel now?"

"I'll be fine," he said, more bravely than he felt.

"Aye, well maybe you'd better lie still a little while longer." She paused, "What's your name?"

"Jamie Douglas."

"I'm Kate McLeod. Why were you fighting that boy? He's a real bruiser."

"I don't care, I'm going to look for him and when I find him, I'll beat him. He stole my father's best shirt."

Kate laughed. "Go on now, Jamie, you'll never beat that boy. Just look at you. You're as scrawny as a highland chicken. And you're no fighter, anyone can see that. The boy was just playing with you."

Jamie struggled to sit up, planning to thank Kate and get away. He did not like being compared to a highland chicken by anyone.

"Don't take it hard, Jamie, maybe the Lord gave you brains instead of brawn. I've got your shirt and coat, no point in losing them too." Kate handed Jamie his things.

"I can manage," he said quickly and pulled on his clothes. But when he tried to stand, he swayed and crumbled to the ground. Kate helped him to his feet. As soon as he was up, he snatched his arm away.

"I see you can manage, then, Jamie. I'd better go. My father will be looking for me, no doubt."

As Kate turned to leave, Jamie realized how ungrateful he was being. "I'm sorry," he said, "I don't mean to be rude."

They walked toward the cove together.

"We're going to Montreal, perhaps on to Upper Canada," Jamie volunteered. "Where are you going, Kate?"

"My father's taking me to Montreal." Her tone was angry.

"Don't you want to go?"

"I liked it in Scotland, but no one asked my opinion. Father decided I should come to the Canadas with him. Did your parents ask you if you wanted to come?"

Jamie looked confused. "Parents don't ask their children things like that."

"No!" Kate paused. "Well, you better be off Jamie. You've still got blood on your face."

"I'll see you again," he blurted out, surprised at his own eagerness.

"I leave by steamer tomorrow." She smiled, then turned and quickly walked away. Jamie watched her go, feeling a mixture of anger at her cool tone and gratitude for her help.

He headed back to his mother and found her folding the clothes and repacking them. She looked hot and tired.

"And where have you been, Jamie? Were you not told to stay and help ..." she broke off as she saw his face. "Whatever has happened to you Jamie?"

He told her about the shirt and now tears streamed down his face. Mrs. Douglas put her arms around him. "Well Jamie, perhaps your father should have sold that shirt? But, oh, he was so proud of it, and I'm proud of you for trying to save it for him. But Jamie, bairn, you're no brawler."

"That's what Kate said."

Jamie explained who Kate was while he and his mother ate some bread and cheese. His mother was curious about a young woman whose father let her wander alone in strange places.

"She sounds kind but head strong," said Mrs. Douglas.

Mr. Douglas had not returned all day. They would have to go to the sheds to look for him and to find a place to spend the night. Together they finished packing the clothes and managed to carry all their belongings.

At the top of the hill they could hear singing and the sound of fiddles. They picked their way through the gathering darkness toward the sheds, guided by torchlight and the noise of the crowds.

Chapter Three

MRS. Douglas and Jamie pushed through the crowds toward the sheds. The buildings were long and roughly built of raw lumber. The windows were uncovered holes cut out of the walls. Jamie and his mother peered into one shed, which was lit by lanterns hanging from the roof. They could see families packed closely together making beds for themselves on the straw-covered dirt floor. The smell of the place made Jamie sick.

"We'll not go in there," said Mrs. Douglas, pulling her head back from the window. "The smell and the crowd is even worse then it was in the ship's hold. And six weeks of that was quite enough for me. We'd best spend the night out here. It looks as though it will be a clear night."

It took them some time to find a space where they would be sheltered from the river's breeze. They spread out their bundles. Jamie gladly sat down. His bruises felt sore and his face and body still ached.

In the crowd, a couple of fiddlers were scraping away at their instruments and here and there men and women spun and danced to the music. Many people in the crowd were drinking, but the soldiers watching them made no effort to interfere. Although he was tired and sore, Jamie began to feel more relaxed as he caught the mood of the dancers.

Mrs. Douglas, however, was anxious and growing angry. "Where is your father? He must know we'll be needing food. I think you had best go look for him, Jamie, while I look after things here." She smiled, "I know you feel poorly, dear, but I don't want to be separated from your father when it grows dark, and he's no idea where we are."

Jamie would have liked to stay where he was, but he agreed with his mother. He dragged himself to his feet and walking past the dancers, pushed his way through a crowd which had gathered to watch two drunken women. They were fighting — rolling about on the ground, shrieking and pulling each other's hair. Jamie watched them for a moment. The fight was more evenly matched than his own fight had been and the spectators were certainly enjoying it more.

Jamie continued on toward a row of booths where food and other supplies were being sold. It wasn't long before he caught sight of his father, standing by one of the booths talking with a tall, heavy-set man. Jamie pushed toward them and called to his father. Mr. Douglas and his companion looked around.

Jamie recognized the man at once. He was the same one who had been collecting bets at the fight.

"Excuse me, father, but mother sent me to find you. She hopes you have some food for us."

"Family duties, eh, Douglas?" the stranger said, his voice loud and hearty. "They come to most of us from time to time."

Mr. Douglas nodded in agreement. Then, noticing Jamie's bruised face, he said, "Jamie, what happened to you?"

"I was in a fight, father."

"Well now, I always thought it took two to make a fight, boy," the stranger boomed, with a laugh. "You've a fine boy there, Douglas, but you've not bred a highland warrior, not by a long way."

"We all have our talents, Johnson," Mr. Douglas said sharply. "What were you fighting about, Jamie?"

Jamie told his father the story, while the man listened. Johnson allowed the cold half-smile to creep back onto his face.

"Well, you tried Jamie, but if you had kept better watch, the shirt might not have been stolen in the first place."

"And if you had been there to help he probably wouldn't have stolen it either," Jamie shot back.

"Don't be impertinent, Jamie, or you'll get a beating from me, too." Mr. Douglas's face flushed with anger.

"Oh well, Douglas, you may have lost your shirt but you have your boy, more or less, whole. And a shirt's nothing in this country, man. By the year's end you'll have a dozen to replace it, and finer too, if you play your cards right."

In the twilight, Jamie could see the look that came over his father's face. It was the one he got whenever he was thinking over a new scheme.

"Father, we must go, please. Mother is waiting."

"Right, Jamie, Let's find your mother. Take this," he handed Jamie a sack. "Mr. Johnson, will you join us for supper?"

"Delighted to do so, Douglas, if I may make a contribution." He reached inside his long linen coat and with a flourish produced a paper wrapped bundle. "I trust you all like roasted chicken."

They walked back toward the sheds together. The fiddles were still playing, but the crowd was quieter. There were many more soldiers, and a group of them surrounded a small cluster of men and women outside the sheds. A short, stout man dressed in a scarlet tunic and dark trousers was examining the people one by one. At a word from him, two soldiers led one of the men away. Jamie could see that an argument was going on between the soldiers and the crowd.

"What's going on there?" Mr. Douglas asked as they stopped to listen.

"I believe it's sick parade, Douglas," said Johnson. "The army sends someone along each evening to make sure no one is in the sheds who should be in the hospital. Just a precaution, you understand."

Johnson spoke casually, but what he said reminded

Jamie why they were here. He stepped back a few paces and stood watching the army doctor at work. In the torchlight, the doctor's face shone as scarlet as his tunic and a forest of ginger whiskers covered half his cheeks. He looked fierce to Jamie, who could hear him shouting at a man, "...to the hospital...."

"I see you're admiring my father."

Jamie turned to find Kate standing beside him. "Your father?"

"Staff Surgeon Angus McLeod," she mimicked her father's way of standing.

"I was just thinking how fierce he looks."

"Oh he is, Jamie, he's quite a bully," she said with disgust.

Before Jamie could reply, Mrs. Douglas joined them. She had seen them stop to watch the commotion. Jamie introduced Kate to his mother.

"Should you be wandering alone, child?" Mrs. Douglas asked.

"My father is on duty this evening ma'am."

"But surely your mother will be concerned about you?"

"I have no mother, Mrs. Douglas. I've lived with my aunts in Scotland since mother died in Calcutta five years ago."

It was a statement of fact, with no appeal for sympathy. Mrs. Douglas murmured something comforting and invited Kate to join them for supper.

It turned into a fine meal which they all relished after their weeks of ship's rations. The chicken was fresh and juicy, the bread crusty on the outside and soft inside. It could be chewed with pleasure, without first being pounded and soaked like ship's biscuit. There were two kinds of cheese and some fresh, unshrivelled apples.

At the end of the meal, Johnson reached into another of his pockets and produced two oranges, which he handed to Kate and Jamie. "From one of my West Indian traders," he said.

Jamie glanced at Kate, who raised her eyebrows slightly. Jamie was afraid he would laugh so he hurriedly thanked Johnson for his gift.

Johnson began to talk about himself. He said he was a trader, dealing between Europe, the West Indies and the Canadas.

"Such wonderful opportunities here, Douglas. A man with your experience and a little capital could soon be rich. This is a growing country, people are pouring into Upper Canada, the forests are coming down, fields and farms are opening up. You'll see rafts of timber coming down the rivers and there's a river of grain flowing too. Why boy, the St. Lawrence has been used for centuries to trade into the heart of the continent. We're going to tap the produce of the heartland and Montreal will be the greatest city on the continent. You are fortunate indeed to have arrived here at this moment. Seize the opportunity to invest in the future, Douglas, and this boy will thank you long after you've gone to your grave."

Mr. Douglas seemed excited by this torrent of

words and it was easy to see which way his thoughts were going. "One needs local knowledge, of course?" he asked.

"Indeed one does, Douglas," Johnson nodded, looking serious. "But it can be had. There are investments to be made; local people willing to consider partnerships and share their knowledge and experience. Of course," he added, his voice growing confidential, "a man must choose his partner carefully, be on the lookout for fraud, trust his knowledge of people. All opportunity has its risks, Douglas, and great opportunities attract sharp characters. If you think of a business venture, Douglas, be sure to find a man you can trust."

"Well, Mr. Johnson, I believe our future lies in hard work and the hope of modest returns. We had our dreams in the old country." Mrs. Douglas spoke firmly but her words hardly stopped the flow of Johnson's talk.

"Why, bless you ma'am, you've left the old country behind you now. This is a new country and it offers you the chance for fresh dreams."

Later, when Johnson rose to leave, Mr. Douglas stood and said, "I'll walk along with you, Johnson. I'll be back shortly, Mary."

As soon as they left, Kate began to laugh. Jamie and his mother watched.

"Oh, please excuse me, Mrs. Douglas," she said at last. "I don't mean to be rude, but the man is such a fool. All that empty talk and phoney claims to being a trader."

"Don't you believe him, Kate?" Jamie asked.

"Did you see his boots, Jamie? And how frayed his trousers were? If he is a trader, I don't think he can be having much success."

"You're a very observant girl, Kate," Mrs. Douglas said.

At that moment, a soldier came pushing through the crowds and called out, "Miss Kate, your father wants you back at the barracks."

Kate rose reluctantly. She thanked the Douglases for her meal and left with the soldier. Mrs. Douglas watched her go, shaking her head slowly. "She's a sharp young woman, all right, Jamie and I must say I think she's right."

Mrs. Douglas spread blankets on the ground, muttering about the damp and the danger of cold. Jamie lay down and wrapped himself in a shawl. He felt himself drifting in and out of sleep, but was awake when his father returned.

"Well, Mary what do you think of Johnson?" Jamie heard his father ask. "He seems a very knowledgeable person."

"We need to know a little more about the country before we can know how knowledgeable he is, James."

"Oh Mary, he's a fine man. He has a stall here but it's just one of his interests; he has trading investments in Montreal, too. Such imagination! We talked a long time about prospects."

"I'll be frank with you James, I do not trust him. What do you really know about him?"

Jamie fell asleep before he heard his father's reply.

Chapter Four

WHEN Jamie woke he was wet with dew. The dampness made him shiver. In the morning light, he could see hundreds of people stretched out asleep. Some were huddled under blankets, but many lay on the bare ground with no other cover than their clothes.

"Good morning, Jamie, did you sleep well your first night in Canada?" Mr. Douglas sat wrapped in a blanket, leaning against the shed wall. Jamie guessed that he'd been awake for awhile and was eager to talk, for he gave Jamie no time to answer his question before continuing.

"Oh, Jamie, I'm sure we've come to the right place at last. Glasgow was no place to grow, either for you or me. We need space and I know that the Canadas will be good to us." His voice rose as he spoke, and Mrs. Douglas began to waken.

"I hope so father, we've come a long way for nothing if it's not."

"Why, are you fearful Jamie?" Mr. Douglas asked. "Didn't you hear Mr. Johnson last night? Surely you don't want to scratch out a living back home when there's so much here?"

"I've no real choice, have I, father? You brought me and I must make the best of it."

"That's very ungrateful, Jamie. I'm doing what's best for us all."

Mrs. Douglas was awake now. Jamie was glad; he rarely spoke so frankly to his father and now that he had, he was surprised how uncertain he felt about emigrating.

"It was Kate's question," he thought. "I've never before thought I had any right to a say in what we did. I just assumed I had to come."

Suddenly, the morning air was split by a high and piercing scream.

"Michael, my Michael, oh someone help us, please," a woman's voice cried.

Jamie and Mr. Douglas jumped up and ran toward a woman who stood screaming and weeping for help. As they drew closer they could see that she was hovering over a man who lay curled on the ground. The crowd that had gathered, held back, leaving a space around the couple, but Mr. Douglas plunged through and knelt by the man. He rolled him onto his back and Jamie could see that the man's face was dark, his cheeks were sunken and his eyes stared sightlessly toward the sky.

"Michael, my Michael, oh look at him sir, just lying there, and last night he was singing and dancing with all the rest of us."

"I'm sorry, ma'am," Mr. Douglas said as he stood up, "I'm afraid he is dead."

The woman fell to her knees, and clutched her husband. The crowd watched silently until two soldiers arrived with a stretcher to take the body away.

"He looks so still," Jamie said to his father. He had never been close to a dead person before and he could not stop staring. The crowd broke up and drifted away.

"Aye, Jamie, he's very still," his father shook his head. "Let's move away from here." Jamie realized that his father was afraid.

They rejoined Mrs. Douglas. "Well James, what was that all about?" she asked.

"It's bad, Mary, very bad," Mr. Douglas spoke in a low voice. "There's a man died in the night and from the look of him, I'd say it was the cholera took him off."

Now Jamie knew why his father was afraid and he felt panic rising inside him. His mother's face turned pale.

"The cholera, right here on this island? Are we to stay and be poisoned by it? Is there no way off this wretched place?"

"Hush, woman! Talk that loud and everyone will

hear you. D'you want to start a panic?"

"I just want us off here. I don't want to be waiting days while they clean our ship. Is there nothing we can do?"

"There may be a way, Mary. I'll be back soon," and Mr. Douglas hurried toward the supply booths.

"Don't worry, mother, I'm sure we'll be safe."

"Oh, child, what do you know of it? What does anyone know of the disease? Only that it kills thousands and no hand can stay it."

Caught by his mother's fears, Jamie looked about him. Everything seemed normal. Families had gathered around small fires and were cooking their breakfasts. Boats were bringing new immigrants from the ships to the shore and the hustle and bustle of hundreds of people filled the air. The spot where a man lay dead, only minutes ago, had disappeared under the feet of passersby.

"It's not real," Jamie thought. "A man is forgotten so soon, and the disease that killed him is still poisoning the air all around us." He wanted to run away, but if the air on the island was poisoned where could he run? He was trapped. They were all trapped.

When Mr. Douglas returned, he was excited. "Bring our things," he whispered, "and come along."

"Where to?" Jamie asked.

"Johnson says he knows of a steamer about to leave for Montreal. He says it's full, but he'll have a word with the captain to see if he can get us on. I had to give him five pounds to sweeten the captain."

"Well, if it gets us away from here, it will be money well spent, James," Mrs. Douglas remarked.

Johnson was waiting for them at the booths. He bowed stiffly to Mrs. Douglas, touching the brim of his tall hat.

"Ma'am, Douglas. Good news! The steamer is about to leave and the captain, a personal friend of mine, most fortunately has agreed to find a place for you. I fear, however, that he demands another two sovereigns in passage money for the boy."

Jamie watched as his father pulled out his purse and handed over the two gold coins. Now his father had paid almost as much for their passage to Montreal as he had paid to bring them to the Canadas.

"The man must be a rogue, Mr. Johnson, to take advantage of people at a time like this," Mrs. Douglas said angrily, as they hurried along the narrow path that led from the booths to a small bay.

"Indeed ma'am," Johnson puffed, winded by the pace that Mr. Douglas was setting, "but I fear... such times... rogues flourish... fear ma'am... brings out the best... and worst in people."

A small steamer lay at anchor in the bay. The decks were already crowded with passengers and the boat rode low in the water. The Douglases scrambled into a rowboat on the beach and the boatmen pushed off as soon as they were settled. Johnson bowed to them and waved.

"Adieu, ma'am. I trust we shall soon meet again in Montreal. God speed."

Jamie watched Johnson standing on the beach. Suddenly he realized something was wrong.

"Mother," he whispered, "he didn't give father's money to the boatman."

Mrs. Douglas turned to look at Johnson. "Perhaps he has some other arrangement," she replied, but she looked doubtful.

There was no time to think about it as the rowboat came alongside the steamer. The Douglases were helped aboard. It was nearly an hour before the steamer hoisted anchor and got under way. As Grosse Isle faded into the distance, and the ships at anchor grew smaller, Jamie felt more and more relieved. The same sense of relief affected the other passengers, and as the over loaded boat moved into the river, people broke into song. Occasionally, a large wave would break over the bow and wet the passengers. Each burst of spray brought shouts of laughter. At the stern, the Douglases were protected from the spray, but the wind sometimes caught the smoke from the stack and blew it down over them. The smoke made their eyes water and occasionally hot sparks scorched their skin. No one complained. Jamie was happy to sit still and glad to eat the food that his mother carefully handed out from her sack. Someone began to play a fiddle.

lways music," Jamie thought, and as
-danced in their small spaces on the deck,

st like a summer cruise at home on the River
Cly his mother said.

Although it was pleasant to sit in the sun, Jamie grew restless and after awhile, when both his parents were dozing, he slipped away to explore the steamer.

All the passengers travelled on deck and Jamie had to work his way between them to get toward the bow and along the starboard side. From there he could see a large hill looming high over the river. A great castle at its top dominated the scene. "So that's Quebec," Jamie thought, excited at seeing the town he had read about at school.

Glancing away from the town, he saw a short stout man in a scarlet tunic standing at the rail beside a girl.

"Kate!" he shouted, wriggling his way between the passengers to her side.

"And who is this rowdy young man, Kate?" the surgeon asked.

"Jamie Douglas, father. We met on the island."

Jamie said hello, but the army officer merely grunted and turned back to look at the view.

"What are you doing here, Jamie?" she whispered.

"We got passage off the island. My father was afraid of the cholera there."

"Look, Kate," the surgeon interrupted, pointing to the shore, "that path over there must be the one

Wolfe used in his conquest. And those must be the Plains of Abraham."

They looked to where he was pointing and they could see that the plain was dotted with white tents. Crowds of people thronged between the tents.

"It looks like a fair, father."

"It's not that," a boatman said, stopping as he walked by. "It's a camp for immigrants like you and for the poor people put out of their homes by the Board of Health. It's been there all summer since the cholera began. That was a time, I tell you. Nothing moved on the river for weeks — couldn't get a man to work the boats, y'see. All's back to normal now, though there's still plenty dying of it. You should get one of these, best protection there is — camphor."

He showed them a small sack which he wore on a string around his neck. "Some swear by garlic, but this has worked for me."

McLeod had been growing more and more agitated as the boatman spoke and now he exploded. "Arrant rubbish, man, mere superstition, garlic, camphor, why you'll be using tongue of bat and eye of newt, next. There's nothing to do with the cholera but trust yourself to a regular doctor and his skills."

"Begging your pardon, sir," the sailor said mildly, "but it's my experience that the doctors here can't do a thing for the disease. Leastways, none but Doctor Ayres."

"And who might he be?"

"Now that's hard to say, sir. Strange man, he is. Came into town, no one knows from where, just after the epidemic began. Did wonders with cases no doctors could help and now, why he's a saint to some."

"No doubt he has a secret formula for some great price," McLeod said sarcastically.

"He does have his own way of doing things, that's certain, but he charges not a penny to those he helps. And that's something no other doctor does, sir." With a mocking emphasis on the last word, the boatman moved on.

Surgeon McLeod spluttered for a few moments before calming down. "There's always someone will take advantage of gullible people in a crisis. Cholera needs the knife, opium and calomel. Bleed and purge, that's the way we do things in India and no one has more experience." He pushed out his chest and turned back to the view. Kate and Jamie moved away from him.

"Your father seems to know a lot about the disease," Jamie said. "Does that mean people are worrying too much about it?"

"Father knows nothing," Kate said fiercely, between clenched teeth. "He talks so knowingly but he is ignorant."

Jamie was shocked at the way she spoke.

"How can you say that about your own father?"

"Because it's true, Jamie. He's an army surgeon; he can cut off your arm or leg quick as a flash but he's no idea of what to do with people who are sick. That's how he killed my mother."

"Kate! What do you mean?"

"In Calcutta, when I was nine-years-old, mamma caught a fever of some sort and by the time my father had finished bleeding and dosing her she was too weak to live."

Jamie was stunned. He stood silently watching Kate's face which was flushed with anger.

"What can I say to her," he thought, feeling a need to comfort her but not knowing how.

"Now I've shocked you, Jamie," she said, with a quick laugh. Her familiar cool tone came back to her voice. "Do you never think bad things about your parents?"

"Sometimes I think father's a bit lazy, and I get angry at him, but nothing more."

"Then you've been luckier than I, Jamie."

Kate's father called her back to his side, so Jamie went back to his parents. He could not put the conversation with Kate out of his mind. She spoke so confidently, even in her anger. Jamie had never thought about his own parents, except that he loved them and he knew they loved him. His father was a dreamer, which caused problems for his mother and kept the family poor, but Jamie never thought to hate him.

The sun was going down, and Jamie found himself watching his parents and thinking about their future in Montreal. None of the Douglases had thought of farming, neither Jamie nor his father were suited to that. Mrs. Douglas had hoped they would find jobs in a trading house or perhaps they would buy a shop like the one they had run in Glasgow. But his father already had grander dreams. "He's never really finished anything he's started," Jamie thought. It was a disturbing realization, so many miles from home.

Jamie tried to put everything out of his head as he helped his mother prepare their blankets for the night. Mrs. Douglas, at least, could still make Jamie feel secure as she moved about in her familiar way.

It was uncomfortable lying on the hard deck, listening to the thumping of the engine. Jamie watched the bright stars in the sky and his thoughts turned back to Kate. "How dreadful it would be to hate your father so fiercely. I'm glad I can get along with mine."

His thoughts kept him awake. Jamie twisted and turned as the deck seemed to grow harder and harder. At last he could stand it no longer. He slipped quietly from his blankets, and picked his way among the sleeping passengers toward the deckhouse. There he might find someone to talk to.

The sound of talk and laughter came through an open window and when he looked in he could see four boatmen sitting around a small table playing cards. Glasses and blue brandy bottles were at their elbows, and the smoke from their pipes curled thickly in the air. Jamie knew no one was going to invite him inside. As he turned away, he heard one of the men say, "Gold! That's too rich for me."

"Well, my friend, there are many times when one must back one's judgement to the limit."

There was something familiar about the second voice. Jamie stopped and turned back to the window. From where he stood, he could see a fifth player tucked snugly into a corner of the cabin, in the shadows.

"Speculate to accumulate, gentlemen," the voice said. The man threw down his cards and leaned forward into the light to gather the money. It was Johnson!

Chapter Five

"BUT I saw him," Jamie said.

"Then show me," Mr. Douglas insisted and led the way to the deckhouse.

It was morning and Jamie had spent most of the night awake, wondering about Johnson. But now, when he looked through the deckhouse window, the room was empty and the table bare.

"There, Jamie," his father laughed, "you've been imagining things. Why would Johnson bid us goodbye and then hide from us on this very steamer? It makes no sense."

"Well, father, I believe he stole our passage money."

"Now, Jamie, be careful what you say."

"But father, when we left the island, Johnson didn't give your money to the boatman, and last night I saw him gambling with gold."

"I insist that you stop this talk, Jamie. I want no more of your insinuations about Mr. Johnson. You've had a lot of excitement recently and I will overlook your rudeness, but you must say no more."

Jamie gave up. Maybe it was no use talking to his father.

Later in the day, he saw Kate standing alone by the deckhouse. She listened quietly to his story.

"Why doesn't your father believe you? Does he trust Johnson that much?"

"I think he does, Kate. He got quite angry when I suggested that Johnson stole our money."

Kate and Jamie spent most of the day together. Kate was determined to keep out of her father's company as much as possible.

"But what will you do in Montreal?" Jamie asked her.

"We'll stay at a hotel for a day or so until father rents a house for us. I'm hoping that his duties will keep him busy and soon the school year will start and I will go to live away from home."

"Why did he bring you with him if you're just to be sent away to school?"

"Because he thought my aunts were spoiling me and he said I needed discipline."

"Don't you like him at all? I mean, do you ever like being with him?"

"Not really, Jamie."

Jamie let it go at that, although it seemed a very bleak prospect for the two McLeods together in Montreal.

It was almost dusk when the steamer neared Montreal and reluctantly Kate went to find her father. Jamie grew excited as the boat approached the quay and the end of their long journey. "At least it's a decent sized town," he thought, remembering his disappointment at the first sight of Grosse Isle. The town stretched from the water's edge to the foot of a low, wooded mountain. A mass of houses lay jumbled together. The largest building was a cathedral which soared over the smaller buildings. Near the river he could see some warehouses and at the quay a few shops. The quay was crowded with people watching the boat arrive. Some of those waiting were waving to friends standing at the boat's rails.

"Now that would be the way to arrive," Jamie thought. "To be met by friends and whisked away in a coach to some fine house where we would eat a huge meal and sleep in a real bed with clean bedding."

He was planning the meal he would like to eat when his father came hurrying up.

The Douglases joined the other passengers pushing down the gang-plank. Swept along by the crowd they struggled toward the quay. In the bustle Jamie had no chance to look around for Kate. They hadn't said goodbye, but surely they'd meet again. Other boats were also unloading and the quay was crowded. The commotion and confusion were exciting and Jamie looked around eagerly. Suddenly, the crowd parted leaving room for two sailors to pass. They carried a plank with a man on it and hurried to the road where a cart stood waiting. The driver sat hunched on the seat, the reins loose in his hands and a yellow flag fluttering over his head.

"Anymore?" the driver said, after the sailors had put the man into the cart. They shook their heads and the driver drove away.

"What was that, father?" Jamie asked, although he already knew the answer.

"It's the cholera cart, Jamie. He's for the hospital or the graveyard, not that it makes much difference, poor devil."

No one went to the hospital unless they were nearly dead, and few came out alive. No wonder soldiers were needed to take people to the hospital on Grosse Isle.

Mrs. Douglas was about to speak when a stranger came up to them.

"Good evening, sir, good evening ma'am. Welcome to Montreal, a fine city on a fine evening. I am myself from the old country and I assure you that you have nothing to fear from the cholera. The worst is over, the disease is on the retreat and you can look forward to a long and, I trust, happy stay." The whole speech was delivered in a rich Scots accent, and when he had finished the man bowed and raised his battered hat.

"Good evening to you, sir," Mr. Douglas said, staring with curiosity at the man.

"Now, you gentlefolk have just arrived, I see. Do you have a place to rest your heads on your first night in our city? If you do not, I can recommend some fine accommodation not too far from here."

"At a price, no doubt," Mr. Douglas laughed.

"Why sir, no charge to you at all," the stranger smiled and spread his hands wide. "I'll not deny that certain landlords pay me a small sum just to draw the attention of newcomers to their fine, reasonably-priced rooms. And you know ma'am," he said, turning to Mrs. Douglas, "rooms are not easy to find. So many people arriving, the city is bulging, ma'am — bulging."

"Well, James, it is true that we've nowhere fixed."

"Right you are man, show us your rooms," Mr. Douglas laughed.

"Gladly sir, gladly, just follow me," and the man bobbed and smiled as the Douglases picked up their bags and prepared to follow him.

As he turned to follow his parents, Jamie saw Johnson hurrying away from the waterside toward the road.

"Father, look, look! There he is, it's Mr. Johnson, look."

But by the time his father turned, Johnson was lost in the crowd.

"More shadows, Jamie. Just come along and hurry."

Their guide led them from the quay and up a dark alley. The houses pressed in close and high on both sides. Jamie's feet slipped on mud and he stepped into a puddle of cold slimy water. The air in the alley was foul. They were all glad to escape into a broader street. Here, one or two shops were open and the light from the doorways helped passersby to pick their way over the uneven sidewalk, but the air was still as foul as in the alley.

"Do all your streets smell as horribly as this one?" Mr. Douglas asked their guide.

"Why no sir, no indeed. But this is Craig Street, sir — and a very bad one it is, too, on account of there's a ditch runs right through it and people throw all sorts of rubbish in there. The magistrates do nothing to clean it sir, nothing at all."

They walked slowly along the street. In front of many houses, barrels of tar had been set on fire. Red and yellow flames were shooting into the darkness and great clouds of thick black smoke poured from the fires. The smoke smelt sharp and covered the stench of the ditch.

"It's good to see them making some efforts to clean the air," said Mrs. Douglas. "I believe the streets here are even dirtier than in Glasgow."

They reached a corner where a large crowd stood in the road outside of a shop. Through the brightly lit window, Jamie could see that the shop was filled with people. Those at the back were pushing to get further inside and there was a lot of shouting.

"They must be giving something away in there," Mr. Douglas said, stopping to look.

“’Tis the depot sir, for them that needs help before the doctor comes. The Board of Health gives out medicines and such, and sends doctors.”

Then Jamie noticed the yellow flag which hung over the shop door. “Is it for the cholera?” he asked.

“Right, young man. But you don’t want to worry yourself about that.”

“You said that the epidemic is nearly gone,” Mrs. Douglas’s voice was sharp. “There seems to be business enough for the Board to do.”

Before the guide could reply, shouts went up from the crowd. “Ayres, Ayres, he’s coming, he’ll help!”

Some of the men broke away and began running down the street. They surrounded a man, jostling each other and tugging at his clothes. The man seemed immensely tall to Jamie. His long body was bone thin and his arms stuck out at awkward angles. As he walked toward the Douglases, Jamie could see that the man had a great hooked nose, yellow skin and deeply sunken, large eyes. His tangled hair, hanging down to his shoulders, stuck out from under a battered black hat and the many coats which he wore were ragged. They reached almost to his ankles, which showed white between the bottom of his trousers and the top of his boots.

“He’s like a scarecrow that’s just learned to walk,” Jamie thought. He began to laugh, but at that moment the stranger turned and stared straight at him. The man seemed to Jamie to be looking right through him. Jamie had to look away.

"Yes, yes, don't worry, my friends, I will do what I can to help you all."

"What was that all about?" Mr. Douglas said.

"Oh, that was Dr. Ayres. A saint he is, and the only one who can help those poor souls who take the cholera."

"He hardly seems a success, to judge by his appearance," Mr. Douglas said sarcastically.

"But it's said he can work miracles," Jamie thought. "At least that's what the man on the steamer said."

Their guide was walking on again and Jamie had to run to keep up. They turned corner after corner and finally the man announced, "Rue St. Denis, good lodgings at the third house on the left."

"But the odour..." Mrs. Douglas protested, "there's no air and the street is filthy. I fear it's a dangerous place to be with the cholera around."

"Now, Mary, it's late. This had best do us for now; we can look for better tomorrow, in the daylight."

Their guide was talking to a fat woman standing in the door of one of the houses. He waved to them, wished them good night and was gone.

"I've a room on the third floor; shilling a night — in advance," the woman said.

She took the money and led them into the house. The stairway was steep and narrow and the candle which she picked up from a nearby table gave only a feeble yellow light. The house echoed with the noise of people arguing and the sounds of babies and children.

Just as their guide had said, every room seemed to be full. The landlady showed them to the top floor. The tiny attic room was almost filled by a bed and table. There was no room for other furniture. The ceiling came down so low that the woman had to bend as she backed up to show them into the room.

"You can keep the candle… for a penny."

Mr. Douglas reluctantly handed over the coin. The woman poured a dab of wax onto the table, then stuck the candle to it. "Watch your things," she warned, "many thieves in Montreal."

When she had gone, the Douglases stood and looked at each other in the smokey light. Then, one by one, they began to laugh.

"Such great prospects," Jamie gasped.

"A man can dream big dreams," his father laughed.

"Space to grow," said Mrs. Douglas, wiping the tears from her eyes.

At last they grew calmer. There was no soft bed with clean sheets for Jamie. He lay on the floor, once more, wrapped in blankets. His parents climbed into the bed and blew out the candle.

A moment later, Mr. Douglas jumped up, swearing, "Bugs! The bed is alive with them."

"James, it's worse than the ship, I swear it."

"One night, Mary, just one night," Mr. Douglas replied.

Chapter Six

MR. Douglas left early the next morning to look for better lodgings and to begin searching for work. Jamie was left alone to watch their belongings while his mother went to buy food. The house was noisy. People clamoured up and down the stairs. Once a fight broke out on the landing outside and someone crashed against the door.

Jamie sat on the bed, praying that no one would try to get into the room, when he suddenly realised that this was the first time he had been alone since the family had left home months before.

"What would I do if they didn't come back?" he wondered, feeling his stomach knot with fear. He told himself it was silly to think about such things. But the thought returned. "They could have an accident, or get sick, they could even get lost and never find their way back here."

That was a stupid thing to think, he decided; they would not forget the name of the street. Still, the fear stayed with him. He was glad when he heard the sound of his mother's steps on the stairs and he rushed to open the door.

"Such a warm welcome!" Mrs. Douglas smiled. She set a modest breakfast on the table and they stood while eating it.

"Well, Jamie, I'll wait here for your father. You take a look about the town and see if anyone has a job for a boy. Just something to tide you over until we're properly settled. There's a market down near the waterfront. Perhaps there will be work there. Just remember, rue St. Denis, when you want to come back."

"So she worries, too," Jamie thought as he hurried down the stairs and into the street. His spirits lifted in the open air and he felt optimistic for the first time since they had landed. The town was bustling with activity and the roads were jammed with carts and wagons of all kinds.

He wandered down one small street after another. On one street a cart stood outside a house, a yellow flag fluttering beside the driver's seat. A cholera cart! Jamie joined the crowd that had gathered outside the house.

At first he wanted to run away, but he stayed where he was. The small crowd watched silently. Soon, the carter appeared, carrying a young man in his arms.

He laid the body in the cart, jumped to his seat and the cart pulled away.

The crowd scattered and a man walked past Jamie muttering, "Someone ought to do that Aylmer in."

"Aylmer?" Jamie asked.

"Lord Aylmer. It's the governor who's flooding the country with immigrants. They just bring in disease, but Aylmer won't be satisfied till all of us are dead, diseased or starved." The man stalked off.

Jamie was puzzled by what he had heard.

"I thought they wanted us here to help build the country. Why is he so angry about immigrants?"

Every time Jamie passed a shop that looked busy, he stopped to ask for work. Most of the shopkeepers just said no, but one got red in the face and began to shout at him. "Who's going to give you work, boy? There are hundreds of immigrant kids like you looking for work — and most of them a sight brawnier than you. What are we supposed to do with all of you? Come winter you'll be charity cases and we'll have to feed you."

"I don't want charity, sir, I'm willing to work."

"Well, boy, you should have thought a bit more about it before you came. Now be off."

Jamie found his way to the square in front of the cathedral and then turned down the hill toward the river. Perhaps he could find work among the warehouses. Jamie was used to cities and he began to enjoy the bustle of Montreal, especially when he realized that the French he had been forced to study in Glasgow was useful after all. He did not understand everything but he understood enough.

His spirits began to fail after he had been refused work at what seemed like hundreds of places. "It's strange not knowing anyone in this city but my parents," he thought. But then his thoughts flashed to Kate. It was the first time he realized that he would probably never see her again.

"She was a bit strange, but we could have been friends," he said to himself and a great wave of loneliness swept over him. Suddenly, he wanted to be back with his parents.

Jamie left the market square behind and turned onto the waterfront road. It was crowded and busy here and Jamie was pushed into the road where a carter swore at him and flicked him with a whip. Jamie turned up a narrow side street, hoping it would take him to Craig Street and back to the rooming house. Not far ahead two men stood talking. One slapped the other on the shoulder and walked away, while the second turned and entered a building.

"That's Johnson," Jamie whispered to himself. He stopped for a moment and then sneaked toward the door into which Johnson had turned. "Of course, he'd live near the waterfront if he was a trader."

Even as he thought it, Jamie knew he didn't believe Johnson was anything so grand. The doorway was narrow. It opened into a dark hallway which ran through the centre of the building. Jamie stepped inside. The smell was as bad as at rue St. Denis and the noise was much the same. A half-drunken woman pushed past Jamie and headed toward the street.

"Wha' you lookin' for, boy?"

"Mr. Johnson."

"*Mister* Johnson," she snarled.

"You'll find *Mister* Johnson at the back, over the alley an' when you do, you tell him *Mrs.* Reilly wants the rent this week or out he goes. You tell him that."

She stumbled through the doorway leaving Jamie very glad she had no more questions to ask him. He followed her and went down the narrow alley along the side of the house. Suddenly, he saw Johnson at an open window emptying a pan of dirty water. Jamie stopped, then turned and hurried away.

"I've got to tell mother about this," he thought. "I knew Johnson was a fraud and now I'm sure of it. He looks poorer than us. I bet the only trading he does is at the expense of new immigrants."

Jamie wished that he could find Kate as easily as he had found Johnson, and tell her she had been right. It would mean going to every hotel in town but it might be worth trying. He could look for work at the same time. The thought cheered him as he hurried back to rue St. Denis.

Madame Joubert sat in the doorway with a glass of brandy in her hand. Jamie stopped to read a poster that was stuck to the house wall. It was yellowed and dirty and thickly printed in small type. The heading stood out boldly. CHOLERA MORBUS!!

The notice gave instructions on how to keep healthy. It advised people to stay clean and to keep warm and dry, and to avoid alcohol. *In all cases of sickness it is essential that qualified medical attention be procured immediately. Speedy medical aid is the best guarantee of safety.*

"You don't want to read that," the landlady said. "It's so much nonsense."

Jamie nodded. The Board of Health had posted the notice but the street was filthy. He squeezed by the landlady and climbed the stairs.

"Jamie, I'll be so glad to get out of here," his mother greeted him. "I wonder where your father is now? We do seem to spend a lot of time waiting for him." She shook her head wearily, "And how do you like Montreal?"

"Not as much as Glasgow, mother. I didn't expect people to be so rude to strangers."

"Well, Jamie, there are always some who don't like strangers — even in Glasgow," she sighed.

"Maybe it's because I've not been a stranger before."

"Aye, but it's a bit like going to a new school, and Lord knows you've done that a few times since you were small. We'll not be strangers forever."

"I hope that's true, if we're to stay, mother."

"Well, Jamie, you'd best assume we'll stay. We haven't just taken a ferry ride."

It was true enough, Jamie thought, as they sat waiting for his father. He was beginning to realize just how big a step they had taken and how little he had had to say about it. "It's my life, too," he thought.

"Mother," he said after a while, "what did you really think of Mr. Johnson?"

"What a funny question, why do you ask?"

"I saw him today — down near the wharf. He lives in a place worse than this. And he owes rent."

"Now, how would you know that?"

"His landlady told me. She thought I knew him. I saw him gambling on the boat with our money. I think he's a liar and a thief."

"So he may have cheated us of a couple of sovereigns, but he did get us off Grosse Isle. I must say young Kate had him pegged right away; now she was sharp as a pin."

"I wish I'd seen her today, mother. I thought I could go around to the hotels and ask for her while I look for a job."

"That's not a good idea, Jamie."

"Why not? I don't know anyone else in Montreal."

"Her father wouldn't like it and neither would I. Young boys don't go around town enquiring after young girls when the families are not acquainted. It's unseemly, Jamie."

When Mrs. Douglas thought something *unseemly*, it meant she had set her mind firmly against it. Jamie knew better than to say anymore.

"But I might still do it," he thought.

It was early evening when Mr. Douglas returned. They heard him coming up the stairs. He burst into the room, panting heavily. He looked excited and his eyes burned brightly as he stood trying to catch his breath.

"James, are you all right?" Mrs. Douglas moved toward him, "Did you find us new lodgings?"

"No time, my dear." He walked to the bed and sat down hard, as if his legs were suddenly too weak to hold him. "Most extraordinary thing, though. Do you know who I met in town? Johnson! He was at the quay. He'd just come up from Grosse Isle for supplies. What a lucrative business that is. You were quite wrong Jamie; he laughed when I told him your story. He left the island after us. We talked for hours ... business Mary ... opportunities, a man doesn't have to work for anyone but himself ... such chances."

He was speaking more and more rapidly and now he jumped up from the bed. But when he stood, his whole body swayed and Mrs. Douglas had to catch him to prevent him from falling.

"You're not well, James. Come and lie down."

"Perhaps the best ... feel a little dizzy ... the sun perhaps, Mary." He fell onto the bed, and Jamie and his mother took off his boots.

"Oh, Jamie, I hope he hasn't done anything foolish," Mrs. Douglas whispered.

"What's wrong with him, mother?"

"Nothing. He's just a little tired." She spoke too quickly, too decisively, and they looked at one another, each knowing what they were both thinking.

All evening, Mr. Douglas lay on the bed, shifting uneasily in a half sleep. "We should get a doctor," Jamie suggested.

But his mother murmured, "No. No need for that, he'll be well again soon."

As night fell, Mr. Douglas grew quieter and drifted into sleep. Mrs. Douglas kept the landlady out of the room when she came for her shilling. Jamie stretched on the floor and dozed, while his mother paced by the bed.

Mr. Douglas began to thrash about.

"Oh Mary, it hurts. I'm all twisted up inside."

"Jamie, Jamie wake up. Run and find a doctor. Father is ill, hurry," her voice dropped, "I fear he's taken the cholera."

Jamie raced down the stairs and into the dark street. He ran directly to the cholera depot, which seemed less crowded than it had been the night before. He squeezed his way between the people, ignoring the curses and blows thrown at him. For once, being slight helped and he soon worked his way to the counter where two young men were sitting.

"Well, boy, what do you want?" one of the clerks asked.

"It's my father, he needs a doctor quickly, he's very ill."

"It'll be a while. Your name boy and where you're living?"

"Douglas, rue St. Denis, third house on the left

going up the hill."

"Is that a boarding house, landlady very fat?"

"Yes sir."

"The witch!" The man turned to the other clerk. "Madame Joubert, Joseph, would you believe that she's opened up again. I swear the Board will have to nail that door shut to stop her letting rooms." He turned back to Jamie. "Tell your parents to get out as fast as they can. Six people have died there since this epidemic began. Now, take this, give a spoonful every half hour until the doctor comes." The clerk handed Jamie a black bottle.

Jamie turned, pushing through the crowd which parted slightly to let him go. He ran all the way back, splashing through puddles and tripping on loose paving stones, trusting to luck that he would not fall. At the boarding house, Mrs. Douglas stood waiting at the head of the stairs.

"Good boy, Jamie, I didn't think you could be so quick."

All night long they tended Mr. Douglas, trying to force the medicine into his mouth, though often it spilled over his chin and ran onto the pillow. Mr. Douglas groaned with pain as his arms and legs were seized with cramps. Jamie and Mrs. Douglas worked hard, massaging the twisted limbs to ease the pain. The effort made Jamie's own arms and back ache but he would not stop. "If we keep at this, father will be safe," Jamie thought and he refused to think anything else.

It was growing light when they heard someone shouting, "Douglas, Douglas, where are you?"

Jamie ran to open the door. A man came stamping up to their landing and into the attic.

"They never tell me where you people are. I spend half my time hunting, not doctoring. How's the patient?"

"Bad, sir."

"Joubert — they ought to lock the woman up," the doctor said, bending over the bed. "Good God! Get a basin, woman, this man must be bled at once. He's near the collapse."

With shock, Jamie realized that his father's skin was as dark and his face as sunken as that of the man they had seen at Grosse Isle.

"No," he thought, "it can't be. I don't believe it."

He watched the doctor open a case of lancets, choose one, wipe it on his sleeve and then use it to cut into Mr. Douglas's arm. Mrs. Douglas stood holding the jug in which only that morning she had brought home beer.

"Too thick, too thick, come on now, bleed man, bleed. We have to draw blood, woman, it's his only hope — restores circulation and eases congestion." He massaged Mr. Douglas's arm. The blood did not flow but oozed thick drops from the incision. "Well, ma'am, this man must go to the hospital, he's very bad." The doctor began to wrap a bandage around the arm.

"Not the hospital," Mrs. Douglas protested. "I

don't want him to go there, doctor. We can keep him here and nurse him ourselves."

"None of your superstitions, woman. I'll not have him stay here, the place is dangerous for all of you — six deaths. No reason to fear the cholera hospital; it's a better place for him than this. And besides, you've got no choice. The cart will come as soon as I get word to it."

Mr. Douglas lay still now; the bandage stark white against his darkened arm. Tears formed in Mrs. Douglas's eyes and ran down her cheeks but she made no sound as she and Jamie sat by the bed, waiting.

"I'm frightened, mother. What will happen to father? He'll get well, won't he?"

"He's come so far, and he was so excited." She stood and wiped her eyes. "If he's to go, let's prepare him," she said.

"She's talking of him as if he were dead," Jamie thought.

They took off Mr. Douglas's clothes and dressed him in a heavy nightshirt. He neither moved nor made a sound as they struggled to finish the job.

Around his waist, Mr. Douglas was wearing a thick canvas belt which Mrs. Douglas untied and gave to Jamie. "Put it on quickly, Jamie. It's your father's money belt and all we have in the world is in there."

Jamie pulled up his shirt and wrapped the belt around his body. It felt warm and slightly damp. He tucked his shirt back in but the belt was bulky and stood out against his frail body.

"Button your jacket Jamie, cover it up a little."

There was a bang and the door burst open. A man came in. His shoulders were so broad that they seemed to fill the doorway.

"Douglas? Board of Health. You've got one for the hospital."

"Be careful with him," Mrs. Douglas said as the carter bent over the bed. He put his hand on Mr. Douglas's chest, then bent down to put his ear there. A moment later, he straightened up.

"Well, he's gone, missus. Too late for the hospital now, I'll take him straight to the burial ground."

There was silence in the small room. Jamie stared at a huge wart on the carter's face, it seemed to be the only thing he could look at. Mrs. Douglas spoke at last.

"No!" she insisted. "The doctor said he was to go to the hospital."

"Look, missus. I take the live ones to the hospital and the dead ones to the burial ground. Your husband's dead — there's no heart beat."

"You're not the doctor; you can't say he's dead, just like that."

"Well, missus, he ain't alive. I've dealt with hundreds since this all began and I know what's what. Now, I've no time to waste. I'm on public business."

He picked Mr. Douglas off the bed effortlessly, and brushed Jamie and his mother aside when they tried to stop him. The two of them stood speechless with pain and anger as he disappeared down the stairs.

“Quickly, Jamie, if we don’t follow the cart, we won’t even know where that brute is taking your father.”

Together, they ran.

Chapter Seven

NOT many people saw Jamie and Mrs. Douglas as they followed the cart, and most of those who did took no notice. A few crossed themselves as the small procession passed. The carter had left the tailgate hanging and it banged at every bump. Jamie could see his father, as if asleep, lying with his bare feet dangling over the edge of the cart.

"Not even a blanket to cover him," Mrs. Douglas sobbed.

Jamie took her hand, hoping it would make them both feel better. He felt sure that his father would suddenly sit up and demand to know what was happening, but that hope faded as they walked along. Jamie began to blame himself for what had happened.

"It's my fault he died, I know it is," he thought. "I could see that he was ill, really ill, and I didn't do anything. What if I'd gone for the doctor sooner? But they don't come fast enough, anyway."

Then another thought struck him. "Ayres, that's who I should have found; people say he can help anyone. He would have saved father."

Jamie remembered the strange looking man and how people had flocked around him for help, not like the regular doctors people tried to avoid.

"It's all my fault, mother," Jamie burst out. "I should have found Dr. Ayres and brought him for father."

"Now, now, Jamie, that kind of thought does no good. What will be, will be and we must learn to live with what has happened."

The cart was turning off the road into a field. Other carts were stopped there, each with a yellow flag. The drivers, chatting to each other as they worked, were unloading the carts, some of which held two or three bodies.

Jamie and his mother looked at the body in the carter's arms. It did not look like James Douglas any more. The night shirt was the one they had dressed him in, but Jamie suddenly felt that he was looking at a stranger. It was at that moment that he really understood. His father was dead!

"Oh mother," he cried, and they clung to each other in the pale light of early dawn.

"Go on, now," Mrs. Douglas motioned to the carter.

He carried the body across the field toward a long trench. Two men in the trench took the bodies as they were handed down and lay them side by side in a row.

They were working steadily, their job a routine.

"It's all so anonymous, Jamie," Mrs. Douglas said, shaking her head.

The carter walked back toward them and hovered around for a couple of minutes. "Most people tip the carter, missus," he said, holding out his hand.

"Be off with you, you'll have nothing from me," Mrs. Douglas yelled, her face white with anger. The carter merely shrugged and went back to his cart.

"It doesn't really seem like father anymore," Jamie said, as they stood staring into the common grave.

"Well, child, you must take comfort. What you see now are the mortal remains of your father. Try to remember him as he was in life and pray for him in heaven."

An old priest had joined them at the graveside. "May I offer you my sympathy ma'am. It is a terrible time for us all; so many laid to rest without a bell tolled or a service read."

"I never thought I would lay my James to rest in a common grave."

"Perhaps it will comfort you to know, ma'am, that the ground is consecrated. Not like the first days. We had some unpleasant scenes when we were forced to bury the poor people in unhallowed ground. Now at least we can close the graves with dignity."

He asked for Mr. Douglas's name and promised to say a prayer for him. Jamie and his mother thanked the priest and walked quietly, hand in hand, to the road and back toward Montreal.

"I am not going to stay in that room one moment longer," Mrs. Douglas said. They spent the morning on the outskirts of the city where the houses had small gardens, bright with flowers. And after many inquiries, they were directed to the house of a Scots widow who had rooms to let. Mrs. Douglas paid her in advance and said they would return soon with their baggage.

They did not want to go back to rue St. Denis but they had to. They walked down the hill and back among the narrow alleys. When they reached the boarding house, the door was shut and a piece of paper was pasted on it.

Board of Health

These premises are declared a public nuisance. No one is permitted to reside within until further notice

By order.

"That may save someone else's life," Mrs. Douglas said. She pushed open the door. The house was strangely quiet. No one was arguing and no babies were crying. As they climbed the stairs, Jamie and his mother could see that every door was open and every room empty. Like the others, the door to their room was open too. Jamie ran up the last steps. Nothing but the furniture was left. All of their bags and bundles were gone.

Mrs. Douglas ran down the stairs shouting, in vain, for Madame Joubert.

"Perhaps the health wardens took our things," Jamie suggested.

"No, Jamie, they've robbed us of everything."

"Except the belt, mother."

"Thank God for that, at least."

They left rue St. Denis as fast as they could. Jamie was glad to feel the rough canvas of the money belt around his waist. "What if we had lost that, too," he thought and tried to imagine life in the city with no money, no work and his father dead. He remembered the families he had seen in some of the city alleyways, sleeping in the open air because they were too poor to pay for a room anywhere. "It's a cruel place," he thought looking around at the crowds.

Mrs. Douglas had decided to register with the Ladies Beneficient Society and so they headed for the cathedral. She had heard that the society helped widows and orphans and found work for immigrants.

At the cathedral, a woman took their names and address and murmured sympathetically at Mrs. Douglas's story.

"It's shameful what some people will do, it really is. Well, Mrs. Douglas, I will see if the committee can make a special effort to visit you this very evening."

Mrs. Douglas thanked her, and they headed for their new home. They bought food on the way with the last money that Mrs. Douglas had. When Jamie prepared to get money from the belt, she said, "No, Jamie, we'll sort that out in private. I don't want anyone seeing a woman and child carrying so much cash around."

"Is there a lot, mother?"

"Well, your father sold nearly all we had — there

must be sixty pounds or more. Enough to tide us over for a good while, till we're settled."

The news made Jamie feel better as they hurried back to their room. There, with the door shut and the curtain drawn, Jamie took off the belt and handed it to his mother.

"It seems very light," she said as she took it from him and untied it. She looked inside and took out a sheet of paper, then she shook a few coins onto the table. She unfolded the paper and began to read it.

"Oh the fool, the fool," she muttered, letting her head drop onto her arms.

"Mother, mother, what is it?" Jamie felt panic surge through him. For a second, he thought that his mother had collapsed.

"Oh, Jamie, it's another of your father's dreams."

"What do you mean?"

"He's given nearly all our money to that man Johnson." She read from the paper, "It's a partnership agreement, general trade ... equal shares of profit from voyages..."

"But Johnson's a liar and a cheat. I know it," Jamie cried. "We have the paper, mother, somehow we'll get our money back."

Mrs. Douglas began to cry and Jamie began to weep, too. "Oh, this is no good," she said at last, drying her eyes and looking around the room. "We have to live Jamie. I'll make us some supper."

They ate little. Sitting together, Jamie could not tell what his mother was thinking, but he felt himself growing angrier and angrier. He was angry with

Johnson and furious with his father, who had left them in this mess. He no longer blamed himself for his father's death, as his thoughts turned instead to schemes for dealing with Johnson. Nothing he could think of seemed much use to them at the moment.

Later that evening, they heard a carriage draw up to the house. The landlady knocked at their door and three women entered. They were all fashionably dressed; their silk and satin dresses rustled as they filed into the room. Mrs. Douglas offered them chairs, while she and Jamie sat on the bed.

One of the women spoke; the other two sat silently, with their hands folded carefully in their laps.

"You are Mrs. James Douglas, a widow recently arrived from Glasgow?" the woman read from a piece of paper. "We are here on behalf of the Ladies Beneficient Society."

"Yes ma'am."

"You have one son?"

"Yes ma'am."

"You are not expecting another child?"

"No, ma'am."

"You do not appear to be destitute," the woman said, looking about the room.

"Not yet, ma'am, but we have little money. All our possessions have been stolen. If we do not find work, we shall be destitute soon enough."

"Quite. You understand that we must be careful lest people take advantage of our charity. You say you were married?"

"Fourteen years."

"And you have something to prove it?"

"I have told you that all our possessions were stolen. There is only my wedding ring, with fourteen years of wear."

"Quite." The word hung in the air for a long time. "You will understand, Mrs. Douglas, that we find places for our unfortunates in some of the best Christian homes in the city. The children are apprenticed to the leading farmers and tradespeople. There must be no hint of scandal and we must be sure that we are dealing with respectable women."

There was a silence. Jamie watched his mother grow tense with anger. She spoke quietly.

"I came to you for help in finding work for myself and my child. I have lost my husband and all my worldly possessions this very day. I do not expect to be cross-examined and insulted in the name of charity. If that is the price you want, I will not pay it. I must ask you to leave."

"Really, we do not need to apologize to you for doing what our rules require. There are many people only too ready to abuse our charity and we must show some care."

"Please leave," Mrs. Douglas repeated.

"We certainly will not insist upon staying," the woman said and she led the way out.

"Oh Jamie," Mrs. Douglas sighed when the women had left, "it may have been foolish to do that, but how I hate those society women who think they can pry into our lives in return for a bowl of soup. We don't have to put up with it, not if we're down to our last farthing."

"I only hope I can stand up for us as well as you."

"You will, Jamie, I know it."

"I don't," Jamie muttered.

Jamie picked up Johnson's paper from the table and looked at it.

"Let's go out mother," he said. "I think I can find Johnson's boarding house. If we both confront him, I'm sure we will get father's money back."

"Right, Jamie, lead on. Mr. Johnson is in for a surprise."

Jamie led his mother through the dark and stinking streets, following the lights of the grog shops and the smell of the river. It took some time to find the right street but at last Jamie was sure that he had.

"This is the one, mother."

"Stay close, Jamie."

He took his mother's arm as they groped their way along the narrow street to the boarding house. It took a lot of knocking to bring the landlady to the door.

"There's no room here," she snapped.

"We're looking for Mr. Johnson."

"You're not the only ones, but he's not here. Daren't show his face while I'm awake. You'd best look for him at Baptiste's, down on the quay."

They headed back to the waterfront. Jamie spotted Johnson standing outside a tavern, lighting a cigar at a flaming torch by the door.

"Mr. Johnson," Jamie shouted, running toward

him. Johnson turned and began to walk away as the Douglases approached him.

"Good evening, Mr. Johnson, we have some business with you," Mrs. Douglas called.

"I fear you are mistaken ma'am, you have confused me with some other person." He stared right at her with no sign of recognition, then bowed slightly. "Good evening, ma'am."

"Just a moment sir, you know me well enough, and you knew my husband. He joined you in a partnership just yesterday."

"Ma'am, I assure you, I know nothing of partnerships."

"But we have a paper," Jamie said pulling it from his shirt and waving it at Johnson.

"Come along, Jamie. I think we may have to take this matter to the magistrates." As she spoke, Johnson reached out a hand and snatched the paper from Jamie.

"Is this the basis of your case? It's an obvious forgery, the signature is not mine, even the name is not mine." He held the document up to the torch while he examined it. A second later, the paper was ashes, blowing away in the wind. "Good evening, ma'am," he said, bowing and raising his hat mockingly, before walking off into the tavern.

Jamie was stunned. "How could I have been so stupid." Tears of rage filled his eyes. "I just let him take it and burn it in front of me. I'm so stupid."

"Oh, Jamie, what cheek that man has. He robbed your father, leaving us nearly destitute, but see how bravely he can defend himself against widows and children."

"I let him do it," Jamie said miserably, "but I won't let him get away with it. Somehow I'll get our money back."

"Just look at us, a weeping widow and her battered little boy. Well — perhaps not so little," she said, seeing the look on Jamie's face. "Oh, let's go home. I do believe Mrs. McGregor's beds are clean."

The way home took them through a street near the quayside where a small crowd was standing silently outside one of the houses. One or two of the people were praying, the rest stood patiently, as if ready to spend the night on that spot.

"What's happening?" Mrs. Douglas asked one of the women on the edge of the crowd.

"It's the cholera doctor — Ayres. He's inside trying to help some poor soul. May God save him," she said.

Mrs. Douglas seemed thoughtful as they walked on. "Well, the cholera got us into this fix, so cholera had best get us out of it."

Chapter Eight

THE next morning, Mrs. Douglas told Jamie that she had decided to look for work at the cholera hospital.

"They always need help there, Jamie, and I think it's frightful that so many people have no one to turn to but a couple of doctor's apprentices and some drunken nurses. I'm sure I can find a post as matron or housekeeper."

"You can't do that, mother, it's too dangerous. Everyone knows the air in the hospital is dangerous. What if you fall ill and catch the cholera, what will happen to me?" he pleaded. Jamie realized that he was afraid for himself as well as for her.

"I'm sure it's no more dangerous in the hospital than it is outside. Nothing will happen, and when the job is done we'll have a little money to help us through the winter."

Jamie begged her not to go but he could not change her mind, and so they set off for the hospital together.

It was a wooden building much like the sheds at Grosse Isle. A small crowd stood outside the gate watching people go in. No one seemed to be coming out. One woman shouted to Mrs. Douglas, "Keep out of there, lady, or you'll be dead by morning."

"If she's going to work in there, she's no lady." The crowd laughed.

Jamie whirled round, but he could not tell who had spoken. His mother put her hand on his shoulder.

"Never mind, Jamie. Just wait here and I'll be right back."

She disappeared through the gates. Jamie stood and listened to the people talking about the hospital. All of them sounded angry and frightened.

"No one asked us if we wanted the place on our doorsteps," one woman said. "Some fine gentlemen decided it would be done and it was. You can bet they won't open a hospital near their own fine homes."

"We should have burned it down the day it opened."

"No one listens to our sort. The governor and his lot do just what they will. Immigrants and disease, that's all he brings us. Well, he'll learn, one day soon."

"You'd better watch what you say, you could find yourself in trouble with talk like that."

"Why doesn't mother come?" Jamie thought, anxious to be away.

It was some time before she did appear. She hurried out of the building and looked around for Jamie, who waved and ran to her side. "It's bad in there, Jamie, but I hope to make some changes. I'm to start work now but I'll be home before midnight. Try to look after yourself, dear."

She handed him some money, gave him a quick kiss and was gone. Jamie stood there, suddenly feeling very lonely and unsure of what he should do.

"I can't just stand here," he thought. "I'd better look for work, too. It's probably the best thing I can do," and he walked away from the hospital gates and the angry crowd.

Jamie wandered through the streets for most of the morning. No one had a job for him. By midday he was tired, miserable, and feeling even more lonely. He was walking along Bleury when he passed a small shop. He went inside and asked the man at the counter, "Do you have work for a boy, sir?"

Looking up the man said, "No, lad. But I'll give you a penny to run an errand. Take this to rue St. Gabriel. Ask for Stephen Ayres, he's at work in one of the houses." He handed Jamie a penny and a large black bottle. "Hurry now, it's life and death when Ayres is at work."

Jamie took the bottle and ran out of the shop. He had to ask directions several times until he found the right place. A small group stood huddled in the road. People seemed to follow Ayres everywhere, Jamie noticed. "Perhaps they think they'll be safe near him."

He asked someone which house Ayres was in. "Message for Dr. Ayres," he said to the woman who opened the door. Her eyes were red with tears as she motioned him in and pointed down the passage. Jamie ran to the end of the hall.

Ayres was bent over a bed, working. "So you've come," he said in a high nasal voice. "Don't waste time, boy, rub some of that on his legs. Quick now."

Jamie opened the bottle and poured the thick paste. It felt sticky and warm on his hands. He began to massage the man's legs, which were tight and knotted with cramps, just as his father's had been. He rubbed the tight muscles until he began to sweat.

As he worked he could feel the man's muscles begin to relax. The work was hard but Jamie did not stop. As he worked he was carried back to the room at rue St. Denis and before he could stop himself tears were running down his face.

"I reckon you've lost someone to this foul disease, boy." Ayres did not ask it as a question but spoke it as fact. "Your father, I calculate."

They worked on while Jamie told of his father's death and the robberies. Ayres said nothing beyond an occasional grunt or snort.

As Jamie ended his tale, Ayres said, "I calculate this one will live. Time to move on, there's more work to do. You can help me if you will, boy."

When they left the room, the patient's family crowded around Ayres. One of the women caught his large, bony hand and kissed it. He pulled away, awkward and embarrassed.

"No need for that ma'am. You just keep him warm,

give him the potion, rub him if he gets the cramps again. Give him drink. Let nature work."

Ayres forged up the passageway toward the front door, his long arms flapping as he burst into the street. The crowd cheered when he appeared, but he gave no sign that he heard them. Instead he strode off quickly. Jamie had to run to keep pace.

A child ran to meet them. "This way sir, this way. This is the house," she cried. The door was opened as soon as they reached it.

"Come on, boy," Ayres said when Jamie hesitated, and led him inside. The house had two rooms. Only the back room was lit with a candle. A bed almost filled the room, but Jamie was able to squeeze between it and the wall. Ayres handed him a jar and said, "Well, boy, you know what to do."

Jamie was not sure that he did know, but he guessed he should work with this patient as he had with the last. He began at once to massage the woman's legs. They worked in silence for a long time.

Finally Ayres spoke, "We must keep them out of the hospital, boy, keep the doctor's hands off them. There's only a few of them know what to do. Bleed and purge is all the rest know. Nature's the way, boy." His voice was low but he spoke with great force.

"Oh sir, I wish I'd found you for my father. I just watched him get sick, but when the doctor came it was too late. It's my fault, I had heard about you and I didn't do anything."

"There's no sense talking like that, boy. No sense

brooding. You can't know what might have happened. Nor can I."

"But you cure people."

"Nature cures 'em, boy. I just help. But for some it's too late when I get there. Now, work on."

Jamie felt better for what Ayres had said but as he worked the picture of his father lying in that miserable room kept returning. He could see Ayres bustling in, and his father — cured — sitting up and smiling again. "If only it had happened," he thought, trying to drive the picture from his mind. He was now so tired that his arms were shaking as he worked.

"Not so hard, boy. Gently does it. You can't push the cholera out by yourself."

Ayres soon declared that they had done all they could for this patient. They set off to another small house where an anxious family waited behind the door. At the bedside, Ayres seemed to forget time. While he worked, an air of calm flowed from him and filled the room.

As night fell, he said, "Time to rest now. I'm reckoning to eat a bit. Do you have anywhere to go, boy, or do you want to come along?"

It was almost eight o'clock and Jamie knew his mother would not be home for several hours.

"I'd like something to eat," he said.

They stopped at a chophouse on the way to Bleury Street where, as they entered, the owner shouted, "Supper for Dr. Ayres and his friend."

He showed them to a table near the back. "No one

will interrupt you here, sir," he said. Within minutes, the table was loaded with bread, dishes of vegetables and a plate of grilled chops. The landlord brought them two tankards of beer. "Eat heartily, gentlemen, there's more if you need it."

Jamie piled his plate with food and began to eat, savouring each mouthful. The food and beer relaxed him.

Ayres ate very little. He pecked at the food like a crow and took frequent small sips of beer. "I remember when I could eat like you, boy. Seems a long time ago now."

Jamie blushed and put down his knife. "I'm sorry, sir, I didn't mean to be greedy."

"Nonsense, boy, if you're hungry, you must eat and the landlord here is glad to serve me and my friends. You look like a lad that needs feeding."

Ayres said nothing more. He stretched back in his chair, with his long legs reaching out in front of him. Jamie ate the boiled pudding set before him by the landlord.

"When I brought you that bottle, you seemed to be waiting for me," he said.

"Right, boy, when I saw you with your parents, I took a look at you and I thought — now there's a healer. I knew you'd turn up sometime. There are some that are healers and I reckon you're one of them. I calculate you've the touch."

Jamie stopped eating, puzzled by what Ayres was saying. The doctor looked at him and said, "It's like this, boy, there are some that have the power and most that don't. Me, I've got it, and so, I reckon, do you."

"How can you know?"

"Oh there are many ways. I learned for myself one day when I was about your age, a long while ago."

"But how?" Jamie insisted.

"Well, boy, maybe you don't know it, but Nature's got her healers. There's animals that can heal, you know, that's what they do for the others. The mole, now, he's a powerful healer and what he can do is give men his own healing power."

Jamie searched Ayres face for some sign that he was joking. The man, however, looked perfectly serious.

"Oh, it's true enough, boy. It happened to me. It was just at springtime and we were hunting moles in the pasture — we reckoned they had made a mess of it. My dog, he had a lot of terrier in him and he caught a grand old mole. Brought him to me and laid him right in my hand. All chewed he was, and he died right there and then. The moment he did, I felt all his power flow into my own body. That's the only way a mole can pass on his power, he dies in your hand. I've known people kill moles just to get the power, but I don't imagine that would work."

"He must be joking," thought Jamie, "though it's a strange sort of joke and he seems so serious."

"Are you talking about magic powers, sir? Do you believe in magic?"

Ayres sat up and leaned over the table. "I don't call it that, I call it the power of nature. I can heal and I have healed. Something brought me to Montreal this summer. I never intended to come, but I came. And I've healed hundreds right through this epidemic. Doesn't that tell you something?"

"But magic? My father says it's just a lot of old superstition."

"Ah, you're a modern lad, I can see. I bet you believe in the steam engine, boy, all that smoke and steam and power, *thump*, *thump*, *thump*," and he banged his fist on the table with each thump, so that some of the customers turned to look. Jamie was embarrassed and could feel a blush spreading over his face.

"Well, father says steam's the way of the future, the railway engine and the steamboat. He says it won't be long before a steamboat sails all across the Atlantic." Jamie could remember the enthusiasm his father had for all the new inventions which would change the world.

"But what brought you to Canada, boy; it was the wind. That's a force of nature that you'll never change with all your steam engines. I just say that I keep in touch with those forces and you have the chance too, if you take it."

At that, Ayres jumped up to leave. Jamie hurried after.

"If you plan to stay at Bleury Street, you'd best let your mother know, boy. I'm off to sleep for a while,

I'll have many calls tonight."

Jamie thanked him and walked slowly toward the cholera hospital.

"If I am a healer, as he says, why couldn't I help my own father? I touched him often enough. What does all that about moles and steamboats mean," Jamie thought. "If only father were here. He would laugh at the moles and all that talk about the future. But father isn't here and he never will be again." It still did not seem possible.

At the hospital, the street was jammed with carts flying their yellow flags. The carters stood together chatting and tending their horses. "They're like cab drivers, waiting for a fare," Jamie thought. Two men entered the hospital yard pushing a wheelbarrow; a woman lay unconscious in it.

A porter came out of the building and carried her inside. Jamie followed and found himself standing in a long room, lit only by a few lanterns. The room was hot and airless and the smell was so strong that Jamie feared he would choke.

With his hand over his mouth, he made his way down the centre of the room, keeping as far as he could from the straw-filled cots, which were crowded along the walls. Few of the patients had blankets, and some of those twisting with pain had rolled off their cots and lay on the floor. The porter had put the woman he was carrying in an empty corner. In the whole room, Jamie could see only one person who looked liked a nurse and she sat by an empty fireplace drinking from a blue glass bottle.

Jamie found a door at the end of the ward and pushed it open. It led to a small room, and there his mother sat, working at a table.

"It's horrible, mother, horrible. I thought I'd never find you."

"Jamie!" Mrs. Douglas looked up shocked. "What are you doing here? It's a dangerous place and I want you out of it. I said I'd be home by midnight."

Mrs. Douglas's office was hot, but despite the summer heat, a fire, intended to keep the air moving, burned in the fireplace. Mrs. Douglas had a teapot on the table beside her and when she had calmed down she poured Jamie a cup and offered him some bread.

"No thank you, mother, I've had my supper."

"Did you find work, then?"

Jamie told her about Ayres and what he had said about healing powers.

"I don't know whether to believe him, mother."

Mrs. Douglas looked thoughtful. "Well, Jamie, I've heard a lot about Ayres today. Most doctors hate him, but it does seem he can cure some bad cases. I know there are folk that can heal. I remember when I was a girl, Mrs. McIntosh, in the village, could do miracles with a few herbs and laying on of hands."

"It would be wonderful to have a gift like that and help people," Jamie said eagerly.

"It's an awful responsibility, too, Jamie. We could help a lot of those people with some soap and hot water or nurses who didn't drink and run off when they're paid. Brandy and thievery are all most of them think about. I'm glad your father didn't die in here."

"Come home, mother."

"No, Jamie, I'll not run off when there's work to be done. You take good care of yourself. Be sure you don't get too tired. They say it's bad to get too tired. I'll see you when I get home."

"Ayres has a place at the corner of Craig and Bleury. I'm going to go back to help him. Don't worry about me, mother."

She smiled and leaned forward to kiss him. As she did, Jamie noticed a small sack hanging by a cord around her neck. She saw him looking at it and fingered it.

"Camphor, Jamie, they say it helps. Any help is welcome, God knows."

They walked through the ward, where the nurse now lay asleep on the floor, an empty bottle by her side. Jamie turned at the hospital gate and waved to his mother who stood in the lantern light at the door. Then she turned and disappeared inside, leaving Jamie alone in the street.

A wave of fear came over him. "Now don't be silly," he told himself, "she will be safe." It was as if the family had made its sacrifice to the cholera and now should be spared.

"But it doesn't always work like that," he thought. He began to pray as he walked back to Bleury Street, silently reciting all the prayers he had learned since he was a little boy. Surely prayers would help.

Jamie spent the evening with Ayres and it was after midnight when they got back to the shop. He was shaking with tiredness, his arms and back were burning with the effort he had put into the work. Ayres looked at him.

"No more for you tonight, boy. Your mother knows where you are, so sleep here. There's a bed under the counter."

Jamie was glad to do so.

"If I go back to Mrs. McGregor's, I'd only disturb mother and she has to be up early," he thought. In fact, he was glad of an excuse just to lie down. But he was so tired and aching that it was hard to fall asleep. When at last he did, he was disturbed by dreams of his father, of giant moles, and of Johnson running, grinning and clutching a bag of gold.

Chapter Nine

JAMIE awakened the next morning still aching. Ayres lay fast asleep sprawled on a mattress on the floor. His pale skin was etched with hundreds of lines and his half open mouth showed a few yellow teeth. "He looks so old," Jamie thought.

He began to look through the cupboards, hoping to find enough food to make the doctor some breakfast. Although he moved as quietly as he could, Ayres woke.

"What are you looking for, boy?"

"I was hoping to find you some breakfast, sir."

"I don't keep anything here, boy. I get what I need from friends. No one pays me for my work, so there's always someone who will feed me." He stood up while he was speaking and looked through the shop window. "Reckon we'll not eat right now, boy. We're needed already."

A small group of people stood outside the door. They were all poorly dressed; the men, standing with their jacket collars turned up, the women, wrapped in shawls against the morning chill. When Ayres stepped through the door, no one spoke. Ayres seemed to be searching their faces and finally he pointed to a young woman on the edge of the crowd.

"We'll start with you, ma'am," Ayres said. "Show us the way, if you please."

The woman led them down Craig Street. A short distance from the shop they were stopped by a procession headed by a priest in full vestments, and two boys swinging censers that filled the air with clouds of sweet-smelling blue smoke. A dozen men followed, carrying the brilliantly painted image of a saint. Behind them came a serious-faced crowd of men and women all chanting their rosaries. The clicking of the beads filled the air as the procession went by.

Ayres pulled off his hat as the statue was carried past.

"What are they doing?" Jamie whispered.

"Praying, boy! Praying for an end to the pestilence," Ayres replied.

"But that statue and the smoke, what good do they do?"

"Gives them faith, boy, and keeps them in touch with things that have worked for people over many years."

"Father says prayer is enough, without all that popery."

Ayres looked at Jamie out of the corner of his eye. Barely turning his head he murmured, "Father's gone, boy! Question now is what does Jamie think? I calculate he'd best begin to think things out for himself."

Jamie blushed. "It's true," he thought, "I keep saying what father said, but he doesn't say anything anymore — never again."

They had reached the woman's house. It was in an alley narrower and more foul than any Jamie had been in before. In a corner of the room, a man lay on a pile of rags while three small children huddled against the wall. The smallest child ran to his mother when they entered.

Ayres knelt down and gently examined the man, then stood up, wearily. "I'm sorry, ma'am, but your husband is gone. There's nothing I can do for him now."

"I thought as much, doctor. I prayed that I was wrong," the woman replied, standing in the doorway with her children gathered around her.

Jamie followed Ayres out of the room. They walked along the alley without speaking for a while. "So you see, boy, not even the cholera doctor can help them all. If Nature's ready, she takes them; death and life, it's all part of her scheme."

They were off again, following someone else to another house. They went from sick room to sick room. After what Ayres had said about a healing touch, Jamie was surprised to find that as he worked on the cramped and knotted muscles he still had no more powers than he had had the day before.

"What do you expect, boy?" Ayres said when Jamie, shyly, mentioned his disappointment. "Do you expect to feel healing pouring out of your fingers, *thump, thump, thump,* into your patient? D'you want to be a little steam engine? It's slower than that boy, but give it a chance and it'll grow for you."

They worked all morning and into the afternoon before Jamie told Ayres that he wanted to spend the night with his mother.

"Sure enough, boy, you've earned a rest. I'll be glad to see you at Bleury Street when you're ready. You stop off at Dumont's on your way, he'll see you get fed."

Ayres strode off, following the latest messenger, and Jamie went back to the chophouse where he had eaten his first meal with Ayres. They recognized him and fed him well, calling him the little doctor and making him blush. Jamie felt relaxed as he left to walk home.

Yet, as he stepped into the street, he had a sudden memory of Johnson setting fire to his father's partnership agreement. "Why should he get away with it? There must be some way to get our money back," he said to himself angrily.

Jamie hurried down the hill, back to the waterfront and the street where Johnson lived. He was not sure what he would do when he found him but he wanted to face him. Somehow he felt he could shame the cheat into returning their money. He hoped he could do it even though, at that moment, he had no idea how.

Jamie was disappointed when he knocked on Johnson's door. No one answered. The house was quiet, not even the landlady was around to tell him where Johnson might be.

As Jamie turned into the deserted alleyway, he noticed that Johnson's window was wide open. Without stopping to think, he hauled himself up to the window and swung himself over the window sill. He dropped quietly to the floor.

The room was small and filled with a cupboard, some chairs, a chest, a table, and a bed, which was heaped with bedclothes. The room smelled as though it had never been cleaned and reminded Jamie of many of the rooms he had been in recently.

"I'll start with the chest," he thought, and tiptoed across the room.

The chest held some old clothes, and nothing that looked like it might belong to a West Indian trader. He moved to the cupboard where he found some food and a single boot. "Why did he keep that?" Jamie wondered.

As he closed the cupboard door, he heard something. There was a creak, as if someone was walking in the passage outside the room. Jamie froze. Where could he hide? Only under the bed, if there was time. He waited, but no one came in.

"I'm imagining things," he said to himself. "Old houses creak!"

The only other place where Johnson could have hidden money was under the bed. It was Jamie's last hope. He quietly crossed the room and bent to feel under the mattress. It was damp. As he slipped his hand under the mattress, a weight shifted onto his hand. Jamie jumped away.

Johnson lay in the bed, covered by a heap of clothes. Jamie felt his head spin. His knees turned so weak that he wondered if he could stand. He stared in disbelief. "He's been here watching me all the time, just waiting." Jamie's mind raced. "Why doesn't he do something? Maybe he's asleep, and I can get out of here."

Jamie began backing toward the window, all the while expecting a shout, a flurry of bedclothes, and for Johnson to lunge at him. He had reached the window but still nothing happened. Suddenly, everything fell into place. Jamie forced himself to go back to the bed. One look was enough. He recognized the ravages of cholera. He could see Johnson curled on the bed, his face sunken and his skin dark.

"I should go and fetch Ayres," he thought and reached out to touch Johnson's back. The man did not move, but Jamie realized that under his night shirt Johnson was wearing a money belt. Jamie hesitated. "I'll do what I came for." He undid the belt and pulled it from Johnson's body. He pushed the belt into his own shirt and looked straight at Johnson. The man's eyes were staring at him. Jamie was not sure that Johnson could see him or, in fact, recognized him. He backed away from the bed and was about to leave through the window when there was a flurry of excitement outside the house.

"You get him out of here right now. I don't want him dying in my house. I warned him to stay off that island; well now he's to go, quick," a woman was shouting.

"Right you are, missus. We'll have him out of here before you know it. You just shut your door and you won't even see him," a man replied.

Jamie could hear heavy footsteps approaching the room. There was no time to get out the window without being seen and no hope of diving under the bed before the door opened. "Will I be caught standing here like a common thief?" he thought.

The door burst open and a man strode into the room. Jamie stood frozen, his mind a blank.

"Board of Health, sonny! Your father's to go to the hospital."

The man picked Johnson off the bed, while Jamie watched. The carter looked at him and smiled kindly, "Don't worry, sonny, your father will be fine in a little while, you'll see," and he walked from the room.

Jamie followed him from the house, and ducked down the alley. "I did it, I did it, I got our money back. Took it right off him and then walked out — just like that."

Jamie's whole body was shaking and it took him a long time to calm down as he walked through the streets — his thoughts racing.

After a while, he began to worry about what his mother would say.

"Kate would probably say I'd done well, but mother will say my behaviour was unseemly. She'll call it robbery, yet I've only taken back what's ours," he thought defiantly.

He spent a long time thinking about what he had done and wandering through the quiet evening streets. Tired, he finally headed for Mrs. McGregor's and the inevitable confrontation with his mother. She was not at home when he arrived and Mrs. McGregor said that she had not been in all afternoon.

Safely in his room, Jamie put a chair under the door handle and drew the curtains before taking the money belt from his shirt. The belt felt much heavier than his father's. He opened it and tipped it over the bed. The stream of coins seemed to flow for a long time. Jamie counted out the fifty pounds which he thought were his father's, but there was still more. When he had finished counting, there were nearly two hundred pounds on the bed.

"I am a thief," he said out loud.

He put the coins into his father's belt and tied it around his waist.

"He stole it first, so why shouldn't I keep it?" he thought. But he knew his mother would not agree. "What is right?" he wondered.

He moved the chair, opened the curtains and sat down to wait for his mother.

Chapter Ten

JAMIE waited a long time, but his mother did not come.

"Where is she? Why doesn't she come? Can't she send a message?" he thought, nervously pacing around their room. He would have liked to go out for a walk, but he wanted to be home the minute she returned.

At last he lay down on the bed. He drifted off to sleep and dreamed that Johnson was chasing him along the street. As his feet struck the ground they made a curious sound.

Jamie woke suddenly, but the sound continued. Someone was knocking on the door. "Why should mother knock?" he wondered, getting up to open the door.

It was not his mother. It was the landlady and another woman. They came into the room and the stranger said, "Jamie, you must be brave. I have some bad news for you, child." She spoke nervously, plucking at the fringe of the shawl she wore around her shoulders.

Jamie felt sick. He knew what she would say.

"It's your mother, Jamie. She has taken ill. Dr. Lyons is doing all he can, but you had better come to see her before..." and she stopped talking and looked away from him.

"Is she going to die? She is, isn't she?" Jamie cried.

"Now Jamie, Dr. Lyons is there but she is very sick..." again her voice trailed away.

"Go along, Jamie, bairn," Mrs. McGregor broke in, "you had best hurry to see her."

Jamie felt numb. The woman would not answer his questions as he followed her through the dark streets toward the cholera hospital. By the time they reached the hospital, Jamie was frantic and he ran ahead, through the dark ward, into his mother's office.

Mrs. Douglas lay on a low cot which had been set up in one corner of the office. A man was bending over her and, as Jamie watched, he cut into her arm. Blood flowed slowly from the wound into a basin. The doctor looked up.

"Who the devil are you?"

"Jamie Douglas, sir. How is my mother?"

"I'm doing what I can for her, boy. I bled her once, I'm bleeding her again. At least the blood's flowing. Here, hold the bottle and give me a hand."

Jamie crouched by the bedside and looked at his mother, curled on the bed. Her eyes were shut and her breathing was slow and laboured. Her right arm was bandaged, her left one showed the fresh wound.

"Does it help to bleed her so much, sir?"

"Don't ask stupid questions, boy. Leave such matters to those who know," the doctor spoke sharply.

"Oh, Dr. Lyons, I'm so sorry, the boy ran ahead." The woman had come into the room.

"Quite, Mrs. Donovan, now you'd better get him out of here. He's no help to me with his questions."

"Off you go now, son, let the doctor work." The woman pulled Jamie to his feet and then pushed him gently toward the door.

"You can come back when Dr. Lyons leaves," she whispered. "He is rather short-tempered, my dear."

Jamie waited in the ward, listening to the groans of the patients as they tossed about in the squalor and stench of their cots.

"What an awful place to die," Jamie thought. He looked down at his hands and spread his fingers wide, then flexed them. "I'm not going to let her die. If I've got any healing power it will work for her — it must."

It seemed a long time before Dr. Lyons and the woman came out. They were talking together and seemed to have forgotten that Jamie was there as they left the ward. Jamie slipped into his mother's room and knelt by her side. The lantern by the bed was turned low and it was difficult to see. Jamie reached out to touch her, feeling her hot dry skin and the hard knots of her cramped muscles. Slowly, he began to massage her legs trying to remember what Ayres had said in their hours together.

Mrs. Douglas made no sound at first and Jamie began to smooth and knead her cramped legs more firmly. Suddenly, she groaned and retched, a sound that startled and frightened him. Jamie felt frantic and began to massage harder, desperate to break the cramps in his mother's legs and bring her some relief. But nothing happened. No matter how hard he worked, the legs stayed tight and bent. He began to sob, "Please don't die, mother," he gasped. "Don't leave me alone in this place."

Mrs. Douglas groaned and moved her bandaged arms. For a moment, Jamie hoped she had heard and was answering him. But she did not move again and he went back to work, more slowly now because he was growing tired.

"I can't push the cholera out," he said, remembering Ayres' words, "I have to rely on nature."

It seemed that he was there for hours.

"If only father were here," he thought, and then remembered the cart and the open grave. "It's no good," he said, sitting back on his heels. "I've done what I can and it's all useless."

He looked down at his mother, listening to her shallow breathing and holding her hand tightly.

"Why am I wasting time here, I must find Ayres."

He stood up and ran from the room, through the ward and out into the street. He ran to the store on Bleury Street but no one was there. He walked back toward the square in front of the cathedral which loomed huge and black in the moonlight and thought of going in to pray. A priest was coming down the steps and stopped when he saw Jamie.

"Why, boy, what are you doing alone at this time?"

"I'm looking for Stephen Ayres, father."

"So, you've need of him, have you child? I heard he was on rue St. Gabriel a few hours ago."

As fast as he could, Jamie made his way through the dark streets, until he found the crowd which always gathered where Ayres worked. One of them pointed to the house in which Ayres was at work and Jamie went inside.

"Please sir, you must come. It's my mother — she's dying."

"Steady, boy. We've work to do here."

Jamie was stunned. "But it's my mother, sir, you must come to her."

"This child needs our help, boy! And you can help."

Jamie began to massage the child who lay, dark and quiet, on the bed. He had no choice. He wanted to run from the room back to the hospital but something held him by Ayres' side.

"I need his help," he thought, trying to calm himself. The room was silent as Jamie and Ayres worked on the small child. Then suddenly Ayres said, "This gift of yours boy, d'you believe in it?"

"I think so, sir."

"You'd best, boy, you've got to believe it, if it's to work. Trouble is, them you lay your hands on have to believe it too."

"What d'you mean?" Jamie asked.

"Oh, it's all steam engines and science now, Jamie, just like your father used to say. I reckon poor old nature will be tamed for awhile. They'll all be wanting men of science to cure them."

"Won't people want you to help them?"

"Not if they don't believe I can do anything."

"Then our gift's useless. What's the point of having it if it's useless?" Jamie said angrily, afraid for his mother again.

"Ease up, boy, it'll never be useless. But I calculate you'll have to add a bit of doctoring knowledge to it, then people will look to you, that's all."

"But *doctors* are useless, they can't help anyone."

"Times change, boy. There are some who try to work with nature, just as we do. You get a bit of the new science, you see, for folks to believe in, and you can still be a healer."

"But if healing's a gift, why won't it always work?"

"I told you, boy, people have to believe in it. If they lose their faith in natural healing, why we healers will have to offer'em something else."

Jamie felt the body under his hands begin to relax. The child stirred and moaned and Ayres looked across the bed at Jamie. "Seems we've helped another one, Jamie."

"Now, will you please come to my mother?" Jamie pleaded.

"You go along, boy, you don't need me."

Ayres wouldn't go to the hospital, although he walked part of the way with Jamie.

"Go on, boy, you'll come to help me again, I reckon, before I leave Montreal."

Jamie ran back to the hospital. Ayres had seemed so calm and had kept him working when he wanted to return to his mother. And now Ayres would not come with him.

Jamie stopped running suddenly, his whole body grew cold. "Of course. He didn't want me to be at the hospital when she died. That's what's happened to her and he knows it."

Jamie did not want to believe it but there was only one way to find out for sure. He took a deep breath and walked into the hospital. The lanterns had burned out. No one was at work among the patients. Jamie stopped at his mother's door, then turned the handle and opened it.

The lantern still burned on his mother's table. A small pool of light fell on her pillow, which was dark and stained. Mrs. Douglas's hair was loose and tangled around her head, her cheeks were sunken, her skin dark. Jamie knelt at her bedside.

"She's so still," he thought, reaching out to brush the hair from her forehead.

Mrs. Douglas opened her eyes. "Hello, bairn," she whispered.

Chapter Eleven

JAMIE couldn't stop smiling. Mrs. Douglas had spoken to him before drifting off to sleep again. Her voice was low and husky, but it was steady. Jamie sat by the bed looking at his mother and feeling happier than he thought possible.

"I did it, she's going to get well. It wasn't Lyons, it was me. I must have the gift, I must. That's what Ayres knew. He knew she'd get well."

Jamie wanted to run out and find Ayres, but he wouldn't leave his mother until someone came to look after her. He sat and watched her as the light grew brighter in the window.

It was mid-morning when a man entered the room. The stranger stopped when he saw Jamie.

"And who are you?" he asked, with a strong Scottish accent.

"Jamie Douglas, sir. This is my mother."

"I'm Dr. Hall, I've taken over from Lyons. I see he's had his hands on her already." He pointed at the bandages, then knelt to look more closely. "Well, he doesn't seem to have done her too much harm, oddly enough."

Jamie was confused. "It was me who saved her," he said, "I used my healing gift, just like Ayres taught me."

Hall looked up at him. "What do you know of Ayres, laddie?"

"I've been working for him, sir. He's the one who saves people's lives."

"Perhaps so. He's an interesting man. More a magician than a medical man, but he does less harm than Lyons and his sort."

"But aren't you a doctor, sir, like Lyons?" Jamie asked in surprise.

"I hope to God I'm not," Hall barked. "That man's a pompous oaf — no anatomy, no physiology. We've got to drive his sort out of medicine for good."

"Ayres says our kind of healing won't work much longer. He says times are changing."

"Does he now, Jamie. Tell me about that."

Jamie told Hall all that Ayres had said about doctoring. "At least, that's what I think he said. I didn't understand it all."

"He's got a good point. A doctor needs to be a healer and he needs to know how to help nature. I've been a doctor longer than you've been alive, I'll wager, and I still don't know if I've a healer's gift. But I'm going to learn all I can about how bodies work. I studied in Edinburgh and I read about what they're doing in Paris. I'm determined to teach medicine in Montreal."

"Could I learn?"

Hall looked at him for a moment. "I've a couple of apprentices and I may have room for another if he's the right sort. My office is on the square near the seminary. Come and talk to me soon and I'll see if you are the right sort. Now you'd better leave, I've a few things to do here for your mother."

Jamie took a long look at Mrs. Douglas. He kissed her cheek and left the room. There was enough light coming through the small windows now to light the room.

As he neared the door, Jamie heard a voice calling from a dark corner.

"You, boy, come here." The voice was weak but Jamie stopped to peer into the shadows. "Closer, boy, let me get a look at you."

Jamie was puzzled. He moved into the darkness and looked down. A man lay on a straw pallet, his back propped against the wall. His face was thin and drawn, the eyes sunken. Thick pads of bandages were wrapped around each arm and one showed a dark red stain.

"Can I help you, sir?"

"Help me," the man mimicked Jamie's voice, his eyes blazed with hatred.

"Johnson!" Jamie gasped.

"And you're the brat of that snivelling Douglas." Johnson reached out a bandaged arm and made a feeble effort to grab his ankle. Jamie jumped back.

"Now, boy, I was mighty sick when they brought me here, but I recollect seeing you before they carried me off. Was I dreaming boy, were you there?"

Jamie stared at him, but said nothing.

"There's the matter of a belt, boy. I had a belt and I don't have it now. My life's earnings are gone. Was it the carter, boy, or the nurses? I don't reckon it was — do you?"

"Earnings? You steal!" Jamie said defiantly. "You stole my father's money."

"I've no strength to argue, boy. Your father's a fool who hopes for quick returns. He'll get nothing from me."

"You lied to him and cheated him and left us without a penny. I don't know about your belt. This town is full of thieves like you, maybe *they* stole your belt."

Johnson stared at him and made another effort to grab his leg, but Jamie easily avoided him. "I don't believe you, boy, and I won't forget you. When I'm out of here there'll be a settling of accounts. I'll be looking for you, boy, Montreal's not so big."

Johnson leaned back against the wall, and Jamie felt him watching as he ran from the ward and into the open air. He was glad to be out in the sunlight and the fresh air.

"When mother's well maybe we can settle with Johnson. And I'm sure Dr. Hall will take me on as an apprentice. I'll be a doctor and a healer."

Jamie ran out of the hospital yard and up the hill toward Bleury Street. He had to find Ayres and tell him all the news.

As he walked along he realized that the streets in the centre of town looked familiar to him and he began to feel at home in Montreal. He began to whistle as he turned onto Craig Street, and as he passed a hotel, Jamie thought, "Maybe I will even try to find Kate."

Other **Kids Canada Series** titles you will enjoy reading

Goodbye Sarah
by Geoffrey Bilson

"Could this really be Canada? Troops patrolling the streets. Machine guns at key intersections. Daily battles between workers and police. . . . Indeed all this — and worse — happened in Canada in 1919."

"I didn't tell Sarah we were leaving. I couldn't. I knew she wouldn't understand . . . . I hate this. Everything was fine before the strike and now everything is wrong."

A heartbreaking story of two girls who try to hold on to their friendship as the effects of the Winnipeg General Strike pull them apart.

A Proper Acadian
by M.A. Downie and G. Rawlyk

Young Timothy is sent from Boston to live with his dead mother's relatives in Acadia, when his father becomes ill. He grows to love the Acadians, their ways and their land. But when the historic deportation of 1755 begins, Timothy must choose whether to remain with his new family and face an unknown future, or to return to the safety of Boston.

Available in French: Acadien pour de bon

The Tin-Lined Trunk
by Mary Hamilton

Polly Dipple and her brother Jack, two London street kids, are rescued from hunger and cold by Dr. Barnardo, who has founded group homes for children without families. The year is 1887, and Polly and Jack are among the tens of thousands of children who were sent to Canada to work during this time.

This is the story of how they survive the frightening and lonely move to a vast, new country; how they are separated and eventually reunited.

Also available in French: La malle doublée d'étain

The King's Loon
by Mary Alice Downie

Young Andre, an orphan with dreams of grandeur and high adventure stows away on an expedition with Count Frontenac to meet the Iroquois at Katarakouis where a French fort is to be built.

During the voyage, Andre captures a loon and is promised by the Count that he may take it to the King of France. The loon, however, languishes in captivity, and Andre decides to set it free.

At once an adventure story and an insightful tale of a boy growing up.

French text included in the same volume: Un huart pour le Roi

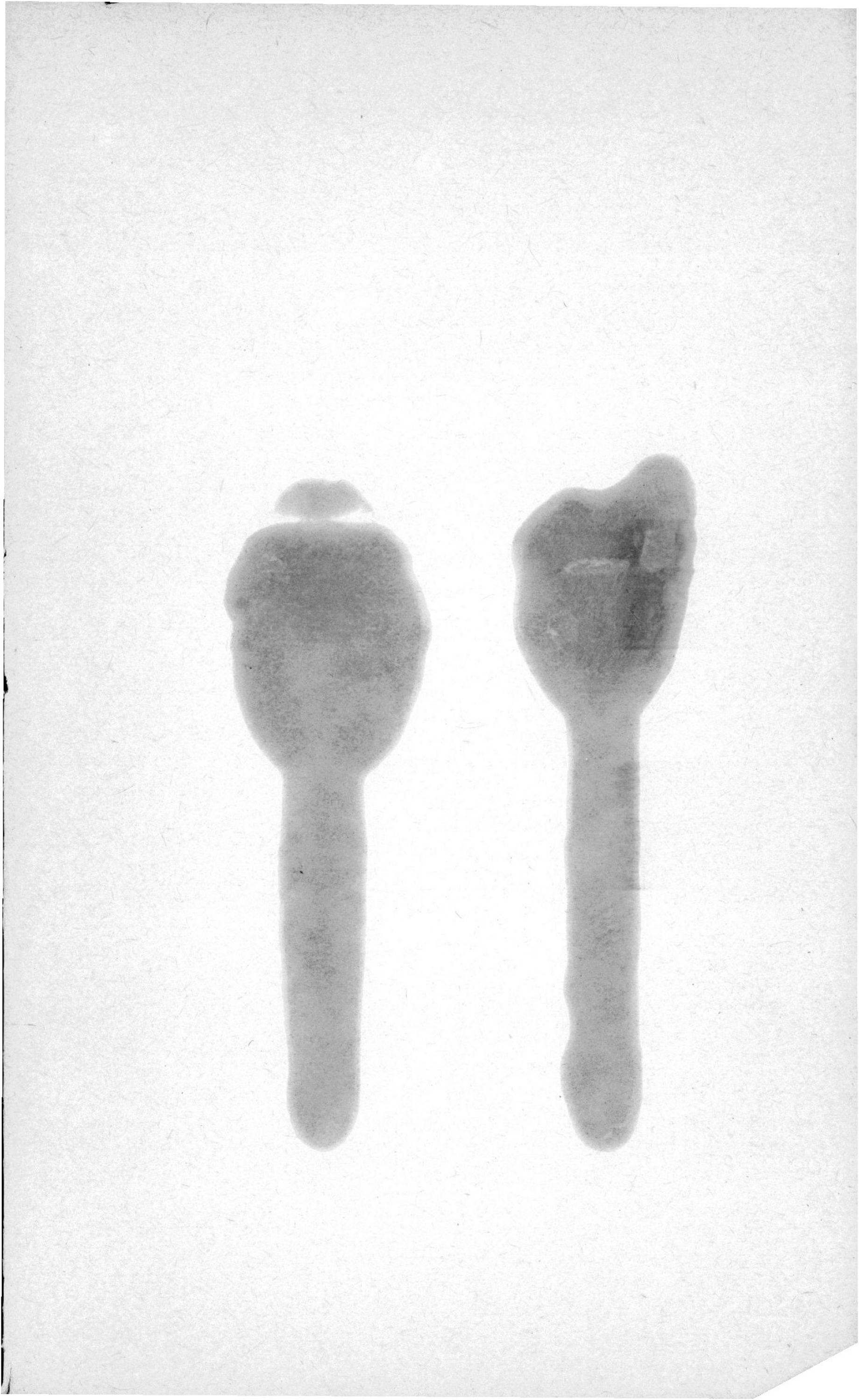